Also by Elizabeth Berg

The Year of Pleasures

The Art of Mending

Say When

True to Form

Ordinary Life: Stories

Never Change

Open House

Escaping into the Open: The Art of Writing True

Until the Real Thing Comes Along

What We Keep

Joy School

The Pull of the Moon

Range of Motion

Talk Before Sleep

Durable Goods

Family Traditions

We Are All
Welcome Here

We Are All Welcome Here

A Novel

Elizabeth Berg

RANDOM HOUSE
New York

This is a work of fiction. Names, characters, places, and incidents are the products of the author's imagination or are used fictitiously. Any resemblance to actual events, locales, or persons, living or dead, is entirely coincidental.

Published in the United States by Random House, an imprint of The Random House Publishing Group, a division of Random House, Inc., New York.

RANDOM HOUSE and colophon are registered trademarks of Random House, Inc.

Grateful acknowledgment is made to RF Entertainment Inc. for permission to reprint an excerpt from the song "The Mercy of the Fallen" by Dar Williams from the album entitled *Beauty and the Rain,* copyright © 2002 by Burning Field Music. All rights reserved. Reprinted by permission.

LIBRARY OF CONGRESS CATALOGING-IN-PUBLICATION DATA

Berg, Elizabeth.
We are all welcome here: a novel / Elizabeth Berg
p. cm.
ISBN 1-4000-6161-X
1. Poliomyelitis—Patients—Fiction. 2. Civil rights movements—Fiction. 3. Mothers and daughters—Fiction. 4. African Americans—Fiction. 5. Race relations—Fiction. 6. Tupelo (Miss.)—Fiction. 7. Caregivers—Fiction. 8. Girls—Fiction. I. Title.
PS3552.E6996W4 2006
813'.54—dc22 2005048956

Printed in the United States of America on acid-free paper

www.atrandom.com

2 4 6 8 9 7 5 3 1

FIRST EDITION

Book design by Dana Leigh Blanchette

For Pat Raming

and

Marianne Raming Burke

There's the wind and the rain
And the mercy of the fallen . . .
There's the weak and the strong
And the many stars that guide us
We have some of them inside us

—Dar Williams,
"The Mercy of the Fallen"

Author's Note

In September 2003, I received a letter from a reader named Marianne Raming Burke, who had an idea for a book she wanted me to write. She began, "I don't know if you ever do this kind of thing. . . ." My first thought was, *I can tell you right now, I don't.* I don't like to take ideas from anyone—it goes best when I work alone.

Marianne went on to say that she would like me to tell the story of her mother. Pat Raming was given up for adoption to parents who died before she was five, so she spent most of her growing-up years in foster homes. She contracted polio when she was twenty-two years old and pregnant with Marianne, and gave birth to her in an iron lung—a medical miracle. Her happiness was tempered by her learning that she would no longer be able to move anything but her head and would require almost continual mechanical assistance in order to breathe.

Pat was divorced by her husband. He offered to adopt out their children before he left, but Pat refused. She spent three years in an iron lung, then came home to raise her family. Later, after thirty years of being away from school, she went back to the classroom and earned a degree so that she could become an addictions counselor. She was also an activist for the disabled.

Impossible for me to attempt this, I thought. *I'm a fiction writer. I would never try to tell someone else's true story.* But Marianne had enclosed a photo of her mother, and I was captivated by the image. It showed a beautiful young woman in a wheelchair wearing a portable respirator, her little curly-haired daughter standing behind her. Both of them were smiling. There was something so strong and clear in that young mother's face; I couldn't stop looking at it. There was not a trace of self-pity there. Instead, there was a kind of joy.

I called Marianne and told her that if I wrote about her mother, the story would be completely fictionalized, that her mother's circumstances would serve only as inspiration for a different story that I made up. I suggested that if she wanted her mother's real story to be told, she should find a nonfiction writer, or she should try to write the book herself. She said she wanted me to do it, in whatever form I chose. I told her I'd try.

Over many months, we exchanged e-mails, mostly with my asking questions about technical matters, although we once got into a discussion about pies. Marianne was remarkably patient and willing to provide me with any information I requested, no matter how intimate that information might be. She told me over and over that she was happy for me to have complete freedom with fictionalizing; her only request was that one "real" thing be represented in the book: her mother's love of Scrabble.

We Are All Welcome Here is indeed fiction, but it is absolutely true in this respect: Pat Raming inspired it. She endured extremely difficult circumstances from the time she was born, but she never lost faith, never lost her desire to learn, her feistiness, her sense of humor, her good looks, or her love of life. It was her spirit I imagined when I created the character of Paige Dunn, and it was in honor of her memory that I attempted this novel in the first place. While writing it, I often felt as though Pat were sitting beside me, urging me on. Say what you will about such supernatural events; I say I felt a presence nearby. I am deeply grateful to Marianne Burke for doing her own kind of urging, for writing to me with a hopeful suggestion that led to the creation of this book.

We Are All
Welcome Here

Prologue

Oftentimes on summer evenings, I would sit outside with my mother and look at the constellations. We lived in a small town, far away from city lights, and our skies were inky black and so thick with stars it felt as though somebody ought to stir them. I would stretch out beside my mother's chair, and she would lean her head back and gaze upward, smiling at Orion's Belt, at the backward question mark of Leo, at the intimate grouping of the seven daughters of Atlas. Sometimes I would pick some of the fragrant grass I lay in to put under her nose. "Ummm!" she would say, every time, and every time there was a depth to her appreciation—and a kind of surprise, too—that made it seem as though she were smelling it for the first time. When I once commented on this, she said, "Well, it might be the last time, you never know. And if you're aware it might be the

last time, it feels like the first time." She was always saying things like that, things you needed to replay in your mind one more time. "Life is the cure for life, and death is the cure for death," for example.

She was a bit of a philosopher in that way, my mother. She was also a bit of a psychic, skilled in reading tarot cards and tea leaves, eerily accurate in random, off-the-cuff predictions. She knew lots of things other mothers didn't: the laws of thermodynamics, how to write a song, the place for chili powder in chocolate, the importance of timing in telling a joke, how to paint Japanese anemones, personality quirks of George Washington. She taught me things about nature and about people's psyches that have served me well my entire life.

She could also make me fear her. Until the age of eighteen, I did exactly what she told me to do—otherwise, she would discipline me in her odd way, by biting my finger, oftentimes so hard it bled. Then she would instruct me on how to disinfect the wound before I covered it with a Band-Aid. She had been a nurse—she could measure with extreme accuracy the degree of your fever by putting her lips to your forehead.

I brought her presents: wildflower bouquets, drawings and stories from my own hand, occasionally something from a store that I had saved for. I never felt the full pleasure of any accomplishment until she had acknowledged it. I was jealous of her attention to others. But I also punched pillows, pretending they were her, and talked between my teeth about her, hard-edged words full of frustration and deep, deep anger.

I played paper dolls at her feet, and she played with me. "Mine wants to go out to dinner tonight," my mother once said. "She wants to wear the fanciest dress she has." I held up the elegant long blue dress, the one used so often the tabs were barely holding on. "No," my mother said. "The pink one." I held it up, the sparkly one that came complete with a white fur stole and diamond bracelet. My mother sighed and said, "Yes, that's the one. Now light me a cigarette." She

took a deep drag, then closed her eyes. I thought I knew what she was seeing: *Herself, in that dress. She pulls the generous yardage in and around her after she is seated in her date's car, and he closes the door carefully after her—she hears the satisfying, muted click. She insulates herself into her stole, breathes in the scent of her perfume, which lingers there. At the restaurant, she orders steak Diane and asparagus with hollandaise sauce. There are gold-tipped matches on each table, and a small lamp, lit romantically. A band is playing for those who want to dance, and my mother does, right after she finishes her second dessert. She will powder her nose, then hit the dance floor and not stop dancing until the band stops and not even then, for she will dance out to the car.*

I did more than fantasize at my mother's feet. I learned to read there. I drew pictures and she explained the subtle art of shading. I conjugated French verbs. I leafed through Sears catalogues, showing her what I would like to have for Christmas, and I painted both our toenails the deep red color she liked best. Once, on a September afternoon when I was six years old, I sat and listened to her patient instructions on how to tie shoes—it took an hour and a half. I was entering first grade the next day, and my mother told me I needed to know how to tie my Buster Browns. And so we sat, me saying, "This way?" and her gently saying, "No. Put the other lace over that one . . . no, the other one . . . that's right." She couldn't show me how; she had to tell me. She had to talk me through everything—how to fold laundry, how to cut meat, how to make the cursive capital *Q,* how to sew a blind hem, how to julienne vegetables, how to fit a bra, how to apply mascara—because the only thing she could move was her head. It was funny, how often I forgot that. Almost everyone who knew her did.

In 1951, when she was twenty-two years old and nine months pregnant with me, my mother contracted polio and was for a time put into an iron lung. I was born there, my dubious claim to fame, pulled out through a "bedpan portal" alive and howling—much to the amazement of the doctor, who had prepared death certificates in advance for both me and my mother—no woman had ever delivered inside a lung, but my mother had been too ill to be taken out of it. As soon as she saw me, wrapped in a white hospital blanket, my hand (my mother insisted) reaching toward her, she rose to joy.

Not so for my father, who left when he learned my mother would not fully recover, that her only progress would be to move to a portable respirator. On his last visit to my mother, he told her that he would take care of getting me adopted out. My mother told him to fuck himself. In those words. She made arrangements to rent a house and hire a caretaker for me, and then she stayed in the lung for three years, driven to survive so that she could come home and raise her daughter as well as any other mother. Or better.

She and I lived in a two-bedroom mill house just north of downtown Tupelo, Mississippi. You know the town. Elvis's birthplace. He had a kind of great luck and then terrible tragedy. For us, it was the opposite.

The sun was barely up when I crept downstairs. I had awakened early again, full of a pulsating need to get out and get things *done,* though if the truth be told, I was not fully certain what those things were. I had recently turned thirteen and was being yanked about by hormones that had me weeping one moment and yelling the next; rapturously practice-kissing the inside of my elbow one moment, then crossing the street to avoid boys the next. I alternated between periods of extreme confidence and bouts of quivering insecurity. Life was curiously exhausting but also exhilarating.

I longed for things I'd never wanted before: clothes that conferred upon the wearer inalienable status, makeup that apparently transformed not only the face but the soul. But mostly I wanted a kind of inner strength that would offer protection against the small-town injustices I had long endured, something that would let me take pride in myself as myself. I focused on making money, because I believed that despite what people said, money *could* buy happiness. I knew beyond knowing that this was the summer I would get that money. All I had to figure out was how.

I crept into the dining room and made sure my mother was sleeping soundly, then slipped out onto the front porch. I wanted to be alone to unravel my restlessness, to soothe myself by making plans for the day being born before me. I stretched, then stood with my hands on my hips to survey the street on this already hot July day. It was dead as usual, no activity seen inside or out of the tiny houses with their sagging porches, their dented mailboxes, their yards mostly gone to dust. I walked down the steps and started for a patch of dandelions growing against the side of the house. I would use them to brighten my desk, where today I would be writing a letter to Sandra Dee. I wrote often to movie stars, letting them know that I, too, was an actress and also a playwright, just in case they might be looking for someone.

I did not get back inside quickly enough, for I heard a car door slam and looked over to see Peacie, her skinny self walking slowly toward our house, swinging her big black purse. She was wearing a red-and-white polka-dot housedress, the great big polka dots that looked like poker chips, and blindingly white ankle socks with her black men's shoes, and inside her purse was the flowered apron she'd put on as soon as she stepped inside. When she left, she'd carry that apron home in a brown paper bag to wash in her own automatic washing machine—she did not like our wringer model.

I ran under the porch, praying she hadn't seen me, wishing I'd known her boyfriend, LaRue, was going to drop her off. If I'd known that, I'd have stayed in the house so that I could have run out and visited with him. LaRue often brought me presents: Moon Pies or Goo-Goo Clusters, Popsicle sticks for the little houses I liked to build, puppets he'd made from socks, and on one memorable occasion, a silver dollar he'd won shooting craps. He could balance a goober on the end of his nose and then flip it into his mouth. He was a highly imaginative dresser; he once wore a tie made from the Sunday comics, for example. He favored electric colors and had white bucks on which he'd drawn intricate designs in black ink. He cooked bacon with brown sugar, chili powder, and pecans—praline bacon, he called it—and it was delicious. He told jokes that I could understand. He drank coffee out of a saucer and made it look elegant.

LaRue tooted his horn to Peacie and drove off. I thought quickly about what my options were and decided to stay hidden and then sneak back in, acting like I'd been inside the house all along—I wasn't ever supposed to leave my mother alone. The unlatched screen door was a problem. That door was always supposed to be kept locked. Otherwise it would stay stubbornly cracked open and flies would be everywhere, big fat metallic blue ones with loud buzzes that made you feel sick when you got them with the swatter—their heavy fall from the window onto the sill, the way they would lie there on their backs, their legs in the air, only half dead. But I'd just say I'd forgotten to latch it—it certainly wouldn't be the first time.

I had only yesterday discovered access to this space under the porch, small and damp and fecund-smelling—cool, too; and in a climate like ours that was not to be undervalued. Mostly I liked how utterly private it was. In addition to my other burgeoning desires, I was beginning to crave privacy. Sometimes I sat at the edge of the bed in my room doing nothing but feeling the absence of interference.

I sucked at the back of my wrist for the salt and watched as Peacie started up the steps, thinking I might reach out, grab her ankle, and give it a yank, thinking of the spectacular fall I might cause, the black purse flying. I often wanted to hurt Peacie, because in my mind she wielded far too much power.

Peacie was still allowed to spank me, using a wooden mixing spoon. She was also allowed to determine which of my misdeeds deserved such punishment, and I believed this was wrong—only a parent should be allowed to do that. But my mother had decided long ago that some battles were worth fighting and some just weren't—if Peacie said I needed a spanking, well, then, I needed a spanking. My mother made up for it later—a treat close to dinnertime, an extra half hour of television, a story from her girlhood, which I always loved—and in the meantime she kept a reliable caregiver. Others came and went; Peacie stayed. And stayed.

Once, when I was six years old and Peacie was sitting at the kitchen table taking her break, her shoes off and her feet up on another chair, I'd crossed my arms and leaned on the table to look closely into her eyes. I'd meant to pull her into a kinder regard for me, to effect an avalanche of regret on her part for her meanness, followed by a fervent resolution to do better by me. She had dragged me to revival meetings; I knew about sudden miracles. But there'd been no getting through to Peacie. She did not tremble and roll her eyes back in her head and then chuckle and pull me to her. Instead, she narrowed her eyes and said, "What you looking at?"

"Nothing," I said. "You."

"Get gone." She picked a piece of tobacco off her tongue and flicked it into the ashtray. The ashtray was one of the few things belonging to my father that we still had; it featured black and red playing cards rimmed with gold. "Go find something entertain yourself."

"But what?" I spoke quietly, my head hanging low. I felt sorry for myself, tragic. I longed for a red cape to fling around myself at this moment. I would cover half my face, and only my soulful eyes would peek out. I had my mother's eyes, a blue so dark they were almost navy, fringed by thick black lashes. "What is there to do?"

"Crank up your voice box; I cain't hear a word you saying."

I straightened. "*What* should I do?"

"You need me to tell you? You ain't got your own brain? Go on outside and make some friends. I ain't never seen such a solitary child. I guess you just too good for everybody."

I stared at my feet, bare and brown, full of calluses of which I was inordinately proud and that were thick enough to let me walk down hot sidewalks without wincing. We had no sidewalks in our neighborhood, but downtown was only a mile away and they had sidewalks. They had everything. A lunch counter at the drugstore that sold cherry Cokes served in glasses with silver metal holders and set out on white paper doilies. They had a department store, a movie house, and especially they had a five-and-dime, which sold things I desired to distraction: Parakeets. Board games. Headbands and barrettes and rhinestone engagement rings and Friendship Garden perfume. Models of palomino horses wearing little bridles and saddles. There were gold heart necklaces featuring your birthstone on which you could have your name engraved. White leather diaries that locked with a real key. Cork-backed drink coasters of which I was unaccountably fond featuring a black-and-gold abstract pattern of what looked like boomerangs.

Peacie dug in her purse for a new pack of Chesterfields, and she did not, as ever, offer me one of the butterscotch candies that were in plain sight there. The actual butterscotch wasn't as yellow as the wrapper, but still.

"I don't think I'm too good for anyone," I said. "But nobody will play with me."

Peacie pulled out a cigarette with her long fingers, lit it with a kitchen match, and blew the smoke out over my head. "Humph. And why do you suppose that is?"

"Because my mother is a third base."

Peacie held still as a photo for one second. Then she took her feet off the chair and slowly leaned over so that her face was next to mine. I could smell the vanilla extract she dabbed behind her ears every morning; I could see the red etching of veins in her eyes. I thought she was going to tell me a secret or quietly laugh—the moment seemed full of a kind of mirthful restraint—and I grinned companionably. "She *is,*" I said, in an effort to prolong and enlarge the moment.

But I had misread Peacie completely, for she reached out to grab me, squeezing my arms tightly. "Don't you never say that again. Don't you never think it, neither!" Her voice was low and terrible. "If I wasn't resting my aching feet, if I wasn't on my well-deserved break, I would get right out this chair and introduce your mouth to a fresh bar of soap." She let me go and put her feet back up on the chair. The ash was long on her cigarette; the smoke undulated upward, uncaring. Peacie would not break from staring at me; in a way, that was worse than the way she'd squeezed me.

I began to cry; I had called my mother a third base rather in the same way I would have called her a brunette. I didn't know exactly what it meant. I knew only that the kids in my neighborhood had once called her that and that it seemed to be funny—it certainly made them laugh. Those kids were all older than I; I was the youngest by three years, so it was doubtful they'd have been interested in playing with me anyway. But they had had a good time calling my mother a third base that day; they had giggled and jostled one another and continued laughing as they walked away.

"You hurt me!" I told Peacie. "I'm telling my mother!"

"If you wake her up," Peacie said, "I'll wear you out like you ain't never been wore out before."

"I wish only Mrs. Gruder would come here because I *hate* you!" My voice cracked, betraying my intention to sound fierce. I walked away, headed for the comfort of the out-of-doors: the high, white clouds, the singing insects, the wildflowers that grew at the base of the telephone poles. Behind me, I heard Peacie say, "I like Mrs. Gruder, too! Um-hum, sure do. Mrs. Gruder, I *like*."

Eleanor Gruder was our current nighttime caretaker, who stayed until ten every evening. She wasn't mean, like Peacie could be, but she wasn't very interesting, either. After she'd put my mother to bed and was waiting for her husband to come and get her, she'd sit on the sofa with her hands folded in her lap, staring out at nothing, a little smile on her face. At those times, she reminded me of Baby McPherson, the retarded girl who used to live in our neighborhood and spent her days sitting out on the top step of her front porch, smiling in the same vacant way, her underpants showing. I would sit in my pajamas waiting with Mrs. Gruder, sometimes reading, sometimes dozing, and then, after her husband pulled up outside the house and honked for her, she would remind me to turn out the porch light and lock the door. Always, I turned out the light—electricity was expensive. But I never locked the front door. If I needed to get out, it would have to be quickly.

Mrs. Gruder was probably in her sixties and to my mind ancient. She was a big, fat, strong woman who liked to comb my hair, which fell to my waist. She did not jerk and pull and mutter like Peacie; rather she was almost worshipful, and so gentle I fell into a kind of starey-eyed hypnosis. She was married to a German man named Otto who gave accordion lessons and would never meet your eye. I had once heard my mother wondering aloud to Peacie about where he *came* from and what in the world he was *doing* here.

Mrs. Gruder was kind, but she made me feel suffocated. She offered me chocolate hearts wrapped in gold foil that came all the way from Munich, but it was the dark, bitter chocolate that I did not like. She read books to me, but her voice was flat and lifeless and she did not make up anything extra, or ask questions about what I thought was going to happen, or dramatize using different voices. These were things my mother always did. Even Peacie would stand still against the doorjamb, dust rag in hand, to hear my mother read.

My mother had perfected speaking in coordination with the rising and falling action of her respirator. She could talk only on exhalation, but most people couldn't tell the difference between it and normal speech. Also, she was able to come out of her "shell," the chest-to-waist casing to which the ventilator hose was attached, for an hour or two at a time. At those times, she practiced what was called frog breathing, using a downward motion on her tongue to force bits of air into her lungs. Seeing my mother out of the shell always gave me a kind of jazzy thrill; she almost looked normal.

Now I crouched silently and watched Peacie's slim ankles as she mounted the sagging steps, one, two, three. I reached out my hand but stopped short of grabbing her. Just before she opened the screen door, she said, "I seen you. Devil."

"I don't care," I called up through the floorboards.

"You'd best get out from under there," she said. "Get stains all over your clothes."

"No!" But I whispered it. I lay on my back and looked at the sunlight knifing its way through the cracks between the floorboards, admiring the way it fell like a series of golden veils. Something could be made of all this. When Suralee got home from shopping with her mother, I would enlist her creative services. We would make this a place where we could talk comfortably about our plans to walk to Memphis.

I finally had a friend. Suralee Halloway—my age almost exactly, our birthdays were one month apart—had moved here in February and lived with her mother, the Divorcée, at the end of the block. Noreen Halloway had hair like Marilyn Monroe, and she had the mole above the finely formed lip, too. But her face was wide and bland, her body short and pudgy, probably due to the divinity she ate before bed every night. She wore high heels and tight skirts and low-cut blouses and jangling bracelets and wide belts that must have been painful. She tottered off to her job as a doctor's receptionist every morning, full of immoderate good cheer, and returned pale and defeated-looking. She would come wordlessly into the house, open a Tab, slip off her shoes, and lie on the sofa reading a magazine, rubbing one foot with the other in a way that drove Suralee crazy. Then Noreen would make dinner, and the dinner was always awful. Suralee liked to eat dinner with us, even if all we were having was fried gizzards, rice, and greens. Little as we had, my mother told her she was welcome anytime—and so was her mother. Not that her mother ever came.

Suralee did not get along with other kids. They could not see her charms. But I did: her very name; her double-jointedness; her new-from-the-box saddle shoes with their bubble-gum-colored soles; her natural curls; the way my mother called her "overly mature"; her wild black dog named Shooter; her artistic ability; the cut-out photos of movie stars she kept on her walls. Most admirable was her skill at playing every one of her parts in our many plays with total sincerity—I *believed* she was a bus driver, a distraught mother, a dead person, a movie star, Jesus of Nazareth. She imitated Peacie perfectly—I thought even Peacie liked it.

I lay down and daydreamed, thought of how I might decorate under the porch, just to get started. I had scarves I could use. I could bring some dishes under here, some playing cards. Old magazines. I could make it an office, a place for Suralee and me to write our plays.

After a while, I heard the screen door squeak open and then Peacie saying, "Didn't I tell you get out from under there?"

I stayed silent.

"Diana?"

I held my breath.

"I know you there and I'm telling you for the last time to get out." She waited, then played her trump card, "And beside that, your mama want you."

I scrambled out from under the porch and pushed past Peacie. "It's 'Your mama *wants* you,' " I said. Peacie pulled the door shut after me and pointedly hooked the latch. "And it's *'besides,'* " I said.

"Says who?"

"Says me."

"That ain't nobody. Wash your hands now, we fixing to eat breakfast. You probably got the ringworm, playing in the dirt like a dog. And no shoes as per usual. You wash up good. I made biscuits, and my sister sent strawberry jam eat with them."

"I want sausage gravy with them."

She stared at me. "You best wash out your ears, too. I ain't hear nobody say nothing 'bout no sausage gravy."

I went into the dining room, my mother's bedroom, to see what she wanted. Peacie had done her makeup well this morning; she was even wearing a little blue eye shadow. She had a red ribbon tied in her short black hair, and she was wearing her gold hoop earrings. She wore a man's white shirt over black pants, and red Keds. I moved over to her chair. "Bend down," she said, and when I did, she kissed my forehead. "Good morning." Her mouth smelled like Ipana toothpaste.

"Good morning."

"Scratch my left arm, will you? Just above the elbow." Although my mother could not move anything below her neck, she could feel everything. I scratched for her until she said, "Good." Then she said, "Are you making trouble already? Did I hear Peacie yelling at you?"

"No, ma'am."

She stared at me, a little smile on her face.

My shoulders sagged. "*Yes.* But it was *her fault.*" I backed up to sit at the foot of my mother's unmade bed. Later, I would have to make it, and God forbid there be a wrinkle anywhere when I was done. Peacie wanted the sheets pulled so tight you could flip a coin off them. "Why do they have to be so *tight*?" I once asked, and Peacie said, "On account I said so, first and foremost. Nextly, it look nice." She sniffed in her high and mighty way and turned away.

"Crazy old fool," I muttered under my breath.

"What'd you say?" she asked, and I said nothing. "That's right," she said. "That's the sum total your opinion."

I'd been making the bed, feeding my mother, helping her with the female urinal, and putting her limbs through range of motion since I was five. Peacie wanted me to start learning more so that we could let Mrs. Gruder go; we'd never really been able to afford her. But if we didn't have her, all of my mother's care from 5 P.M. until when Peacie came at six the next morning would fall to me. I was simply not ready. Nor did I want to be.

I felt it was enough being alone with my mother at night, which I'd been doing since I was ten—information that we went to great lengths to hide from our social worker, Susan Hogart, who was due for another visit any day now. Peacie's sister, Willa, had been instructed that if anyone called her house asking for Janice, she was to assume the role. My mother and Peacie both made references to "Janice" in ways casual and believable whenever Susan came. For my part, after a few cursory exchanges, I was always sent outside to play. My mother told Susan it was because she didn't want anything that came up in their discussions to be upsetting to me, but in fact it was so that I wouldn't reveal the fact that "Janice Peterson" was me.

"Did you hear anything last night?" my mother asked.

"Yes, ma'am. Real loud gunshots over in Shakerag." Peacie lived in Shakerag, a community of Negroes not far from us. I'd never been there, but everybody knew about it. They had their own grocery store there, their own café and juke joint, their own ways.

"It wasn't gunshots," my mother said.

"What was it, then?"

She looked at me, seeming to consider something, then changed her mind.

The noise from Shakerag hadn't bothered me. I always slept lightly at night, getting up a few times to change my mother's position or give her the bedpan or a drink of water—and always fell easily back to sleep to the distant, humming sound of her respirator. Suralee asked me once if it wasn't awful getting up so often at night, and I told her no, privately wondering if it wouldn't be boring sleeping straight through. I had seen things, getting up at various hours of the night: shooting stars, the glowing eyes of an owl or some other animal in the backyard, spectacular dawns, sometimes headlights from the nearby highway, the beams elongated and searching and melancholy. When the wind rustled the trees at night, it bordered on being scary, so there was a coziness to being inside and watching. I liked the nighttime anyway, for its qualities of mystery, drama, even evil; I felt privileged to be able to look at the glowing hands of the alarm clock and see it reading 4:17 A.M. I might not be allowed to drink coffee or wear lipstick or hike my skirts up as high as I wanted them, but I could say with complete honesty that I was up "all hours of the night."

We had an arrangement with Riley Coombs, the old man who lived across the street, whereby if either my mother or I needed someone in an emergency, he would come, but it was of little comfort to me. Riley didn't move very quickly. He didn't hear so well. Luckily, the only time we'd needed him was one winter night when we had a storm and the power went out. My mother hadn't needed to call me; when her respirator stopped, the silence woke me as surely as an alarm clock would have. I raced downstairs to the backup generator, but when I flicked the switch it didn't go on. She told me calmly to go and get Riley. She was able to frog-breathe long enough for him to come over and make the relatively minor adjustment that was required. My mother wanted to pay him, but he refused, standing there in his long johns and unlaced boots and ratty raincoat, his hair sticking out from the sides of his head, his eyes downcast. He would never look at my mother, but he did volunteer himself wholeheartedly to her in this way. He made sure I watched him fix the switch that night, gestured with his chin for me to come and sit beside him while he did it; and there was in his wordlessness a mild admonition: I should have been taught this already.

Apart from that incident, the only times my mother had ever needed me at night on any kind of emergency basis were the rare times when she had a cold and got stuffed up. She would call and I would go down and hold a dishcloth to her nose—tissues were too expensive, and Peacie did laundry so vengefully no germs could possibly survive.

But for the outstanding fact of polio, my mother was remarkably healthy; she suffered an occasional problem requiring hospitalization only once or twice a year; and she always came home in a couple of days. Her nurse's training had come in handy; she knew what to do to prevent problems. (If *I* became ill, Peacie worked overtime. I tended to recover quickly.) Sometimes I would awaken on my own and come to stand at the foot of her bed, watching her sleep, making sure. But that was about comfort more than anxiety. It was like when I got a new toy and slept with it: I awakened then for the joy of simply seeing it, and slept better for having done so. It was an odd pairing-off: my worries that something might happen pitted against my belief that my mother, though paralyzed, could nonetheless handle anything. We were in each other's care in ways simple and profound.

"I want you to change the sheets for me, and then we'll have breakfast," my mother said. "The blue flowered ones are clean."

I sighed quietly and started stripping the bed. Other kids were planning their days, thinking of what to do with their free time. Swimming. Movies. Shopping. Hanging out in bedrooms and listening to new 45s, practicing dances. I had some time, but never a whole day.

"What are you going to do today?" my mother asked. Sometimes it was like she read my mind.

"Suralee's coming over after she's done shopping. We're working on a new play." I would not tell my mother about under the porch; I needed my secrets from her.

"Would you walk to town for me when she comes? I've got enough to give you each money for an ice cream."

I felt immensely better. Suralee and I could get butter-pecan cones at the drugstore and then sit on the floor to look through the magazines: *Photoplay* and *Silver Screen. True Confessions* and *True Romance.* Soon the big thick fall *Seventeen* would arrive. All we had to do was to be careful not to spill anything on the pages or bend them, and we could look for as long as we wanted. Opal Beasley managed the drugstore; she was a grandmotherly type who always inquired after my "dear" mother and patted the top of my head, saying, "Bless your heart." Suralee hated her doing this and often suggested I tell her not to, but I liked it. And I liked how Mrs. Beasley sent her dumb son, Harley, over on his bicycle with blackberry muffins for us, or shoofly pie, or fried chicken, or tomatoes from her garden. We took all donations, never refused a thing. Some people would leave things anonymously in paper bags or boxes on our porch; others made a point of handing us their donations—they were the ones who searched our faces for what they considered the proper display of gratitude.

We didn't keep everything, of course: the moldy shower curtains, underwear, the dresses hopelessly faded and missing buttons and stretched at the seams, the cans of food that had passed their expiration date—those we wrapped in newspaper and threw out in the dead of night. My mother lived in fear that we would be discovered discarding something someone had given us; we were too dependent on offerings to risk offending anyone. We took in dishes, clothes, rugs, linens, food, and toys. We had many board games with missing pieces: I once made dice out of rocks. But our Scrabble game was complete; my mother had gotten it new, and she loved it. We played at least three times a week, and my mother was a stickler: You had to know not only the spelling but the meaning of the word. Except when Peacie played with us. Then my mother bent the rules. Last time we'd played, Peacie had put GUKL on the board. "What's that?" I'd asked. "That's not a word!"

"Is too," Peacie had said, but she wouldn't look me in the eye.

"Oh yeah? Well then, what's it mean?"

"Means a animal lives in the jungle. In Africa. Got the green eyes and yellow fur, stick out all over him." Then she had looked at me, challenging me.

I'd reached for the dictionary but my mother had said, "Let it be, Diana."

"It's not a word!" I said. "She's cheating!"

"I believe I read about that animal in *National Geographic,*" my mother said, and Peacie nodded and rocked, saying, "Um-hum, I *know* you did."

Later, after Peacie had gone home, I'd asked my mother why she had let Peacie cheat. My mother had not answered my question; she'd just told me to clean up from the refreshments we'd had. LaRue had brought us a "portable party," as he'd called it: Coke, chips, dip made with Lipton onion-soup mix and sour cream. Then he'd sat and read one of his yellowing paperback books while the rest of us argued over word definitions.

LaRue was proud of having learned to read—a nephew from his hometown of Meridian had taught him recently. His lips moved and he followed along with his finger when he read; he made it look delicious. I often imitated his style when I read my own books. It made me feel like a preacher man holding a weighty tome with gilded pages and a red ribbon marker.

"Li'l Bit," he called his nephew, who was slight in stature but big in ambition. Li'l Bit had asthma that prevented him from joining the army, so he joined what LaRue called the Movement—he told me Li'l Bit was working all over Neshoba County that summer, helping civil rights workers register blacks. "Now, you find me a big man have that kind of courage," LaRue had said. I wasn't sure why "registering" someone required courage, but I didn't argue. I never argued with him.

He was such a nice man, LaRue Royce, tall and gentle and patient. He moved with an ease that made you feel relaxed to watch him. I'd known him a long time. Peacie used to be a live-in—from the time I came home from the hospital until I was ten, she slept in the living room on our pullout sofa and kept her clothes in the tiny front-hall closet. She had a fake-fur coat, and I used to sit on the floor of the closet with the door closed and suck my thumb while I rubbed that coat under my nose.

When Peacie lived with us, LaRue used to stay over with her sometimes; I would hear them talking and laughing downstairs, and when the talking stopped, other noises began. Once, when I was eight, I'd been successful at sneaking up on them: I saw Peacie lying naked under LaRue with her head thrown back, her mouth open, and LaRue moving rapidly in and out of her. She was saying, "Uh! *Uh!*" and I saw her fingers dig into his shoulders. I snuck back upstairs and lay in bed moving my hips the way I'd seen them do. My mother kept a radio at her bedside that she never turned off. But I was sure she heard them, too. I believe her attitude was that they both deserved their pleasure, and more. We owed them more than we could ever repay.

There was a time, for example, when I was in kindergarten and my mother was in the hospital for a bladder infection and I'd awakened fearing she had just died. Peacie was there, sleeping on the sofa with LaRue, and I went to get her, telling her we had to go to the hospital right away, my mother had died. "She didn't no way die," Peacie said. "She only got a little infection. She be home in a day or two. Meantime I'm gon' take my rest. And I advise you do the same." But I stood insisting that we had to go, weeping, and finally LaRue said he would drive me to the hospital. Peacie said he would do no such thing. LaRue said the child was scared, he would take me to see my mother, it was all right, he didn't mind. Peacie said I was no child, look in my eyes, I was the devil. LaRue laughed and got up to get dressed; Peacie sighed and got up, too.

When we arrived at the hospital, I was taken by a supervising nurse to the floor where my mother was. From there, the nurse caring for my mother took me to stand beside her bed, cautioning me not to awaken her. But I did that very thing immediately, woke her and many other patients, calling loudly, "Mama, Mama, are you dead?" My mother asked the nurse to put me up next to her, and she gave me a kiss. Then she told me to go home, which I did unwillingly. She had a TV in that room, bolted right to the wall. There was air-conditioning there.

When we arrived back home I'd asked Peacie to make me some biscuits. "You want to fall asleep in school tomorrow?" Peacie said. "Go on up to bed and don't be calling no more. Act like your mouth sewn shut. In the morning, you have your breakfast as usual, but for now you got to sleep. And that's the final end of this conversation."

I looked over at LaRue. "Not this time," he said, but he gently tucked me in and sang to me, briefly, before he went back downstairs with Peacie. The feel of his big, warm hand on my forehead, pushing back my hair, that was something.

I threw my mother's dirty sheets into the laundry basket and shook out the new ones. I always liked doing that, for the way they looked like billowing sails, for the way they suggested going far away.

After I finished making the bed, I asked my mother what she needed downtown.

"Milk and cereal," she said. "And the icebox is broken again—it's barely keeping things cool. Go over to the hardware store and see if Brooks is working today."

Sometimes I wondered why we even had a refrigerator. Most times, it held more clothes than food—Peacie kept her sprinkled ironing there in a plastic bag. But the thing broke all the time and then I'd have to go and get Brooks Robbins to fix it, and I didn't like him. He made terrible jokes, and he looked at my mother in a way I found disgusting. "Pretty Paige," he called her, a play on Patti Page. She was still pretty—beautiful, in fact. Her arms were a bit too thin and her hands had a kind of elongated quality now, an eerie unnaturalness that could put you off even if they weren't resting across the top of a hose that went into the center of a portable ventilator. But Brooks had known her before she got polio—since the day she arrived in Tupelo, in fact—and I thought he still saw her as that lovely young woman who was kind to him but would never take him up on his numerous offers to take her out. He retreated in his outright pursuit of her when she married my father—for one thing, Charlie Dunn was a friend of his—but he always flirted with her. These days, he liked to hang around when my mother was outside sunning herself, her legs revealed, resting long and still shapely on the extended rests of her wheelchair. She didn't mind people seeing her. "I'm not ashamed," she would say. "People who think I should be ashamed should be ashamed."

Whenever she sunbathed, my mother wore a turquoise bikini top over her shell, and turquoise shorts beneath it. Peacie had made an extension for the top out of a tie that someone had unthinkingly donated to us, and had stuffed the cups with socks. When she finished sewing them in, she held the top up before my mother for her approval. "What do you think?" she asked.

My mother raised an eyebrow and cocked her head. "Just wear a smile and a Jantzen," she'd said, then added, "A couple more socks wouldn't be a bad idea."

Peacie would plug extension cord into extension cord so that my mother could stay hooked up to her respirator, then push her down the board ramp LaRue had built over one side of the porch steps. She would position the wheelchair just so, and then give my mother sips of sun tea from a tall plastic tumbler. That tumbler had glitter embedded in the plastic, and my mother and I both liked to see it sparkle in the sun. Peacie liked drinking from a Mason jar, and she liked plenty of sugar in her tea. I once watched her spooning it in, and said, "Sugar's expensive, you know." She looked up at me and I felt ashamed. "You can have as much as you want, though," I said, and she answered, "Lordy Lord, Miss Diana, I sho' am grateful for yo' kindness, yes I is." "I'm sorry," I muttered and she said, "Go outside. Miser."

My mother tanned and smoked her cigarettes, leaving behind the red imprint from the lipstick she was never without during her waking hours—many times a day, she would ask, "Is my lipstick on?" Peacie sat beside her on a lawn chair, her shoes off her feet but her stockinged feet resting on top of those shoes—Peacie never went barefoot, claiming it caused epilepsy, among other things. She looked through magazines, holding them so that both she and my mother could see and licking her fingers delicately before she turned each page. When Peacie wanted to know what a story was about, my mother read it to her. Sometimes they would laugh together over something, Peacie's hand over her mouth to cover her missing side tooth, and when I said, "What? What's funny?" they would say, "Oh, nothing," and look at each other and laugh again. My jealousy at such moments made for a dime-sized pocket of heat behind my earlobes.

Last week I had slipped inside the back door where I stood unseen by my mother and Peacie. They were sitting at the kitchen table and my mother was reading tarot cards for Peacie—their heads were bent over the crosslike spread, and they were staring intently at the images. My mother did readings for lots of women—they would come in and pay a dollar to hear what she said, then leave as quickly as possible after the reading, though my mother always invited them to stay for a visit. Oh, they would love to, they always said, but . . . I imagined they figured the dollar was price enough to pay.

I stood where I could see and not be seen. If my mother or Peacie noticed me, they'd make me leave—I knew this from past experience. Both of them regarded what occurred during readings as spiritual, fragile, almost holy. They saw it as being part of this world and of another one, too, one that was parallel and mysterious and reachable only by those with "the gift." They believed my mother was benignly possessed when she read the cards, that she became a conduit for otherwise unknowable truths. Peacie would put the cards into my mother's hands before they were cut; my mother would close her eyes and hold them for varying lengths of time. When she opened her eyes and nodded, Peacie would take the cards and cut the deck at a place my mother approved. Then she would lay out the arrangement my mother dictated.

My mother was talking about LaRue, and the card Peacie had just turned over was *The World.* "Hmmmm," my mother said, "very interesting, considering what you just told me. This card is a journey that leads ultimately to a complete human being. There's a real mix of things suggested here, a kind of battle inside, between opposite ways of being. But the two warring parts have to come together for some inner resolution, first. It's a time of bold admission for him. And a time to gather the courage required to start this journey."

"But will he be safe if he does it?" Peacie asked.

"Turn the next card," my mother said, and then there was a long silence while she studied it. Finally she said, "I can't really say."

"Oh, my sweet Jesus," Peacie said, and began to cry. "I don't know why he got to do this." She turned her head to wipe at her face with her apron, saw me, and jerked erect. "How long you been there?" she said. "Sneaky as a alley cat!"

"I just *got* here," I said. *"What."*

She knew I was lying. I wished her out of my house, out of my life. And though I knew very well its uselessness, I wished again that my mother had never gotten the disease that so unrelentingly dictated the life we led.

They'd been going to have a picnic, my parents. My mother had awakened that Saturday morning feeling more uncomfortable than usual with her advanced pregnancy. In addition to that, it was a blisteringly hot July morning with high humidity. She wanted to get in the car so that she could feel a good breeze—the fans, she said, were like panting dogs. My father laid plastic and then towels on my mother's side of the seat, just in case her water broke. The car, though not new, was new to them, and they both took great pride in it. It was a 1948 Studebaker, banged up a bit on one side, but my parents didn't mind.

They headed out northwest on Highway 78 for the open countryside, and drove for many miles, past Sherman, past New Albany, into the Holly Springs National Forest. My mother loved traveling, loved going away, but not on any planned trip. She liked to just spontaneously take off. As a child, adopted at age six from an orphanage in Oxford, she used to pack her cardboard suitcase with underpants and red licorice and then disappear into the fields behind her farmhouse. Or she would take off walking down the highway her family lived next to, driving her parents to distraction. At fifteen, she began running off with boys, returning at all hours of the night. Finally, at sixteen, her exasperated parents threw her out of the house. They believed that this rash act would make her come to her senses. Instead, she cut off all contact with them, found a job in a Tupelo motel where she ended up living, and two years later married my father. When she became pregnant with me, she found that she wanted to reestablish contact with her mother. But her parents had moved, and she never found them again.

On that July day, my mother pointed to a grassy bank under cottonwood trees next to a running stream just outside Independence. My father parked the car, and my parents took off their shoes and waded in the cold, clear water until their feet were numb. Then they began eating the lunch my mother had packed. But before she was halfway through, my mother began feeling much sicker—her sore throat, nausea, and weakness were worse, and her eyes began to burn. "I believe you're in labor," my father said, and my mother said no, it was the flu, and she really was feeling very bad, could they go home? My father helped her to her feet and she fell against him, telling him she felt dizzy. "Paige, the baby's coming!" my father said, and at this point my mother, who was, remember, a nurse, grew angry. "I'm not in labor!" she told him. Then her anger gave way to fear, and she said, "It's not the flu, either. I don't know what it is, but I'm sick, I'm so sick. You'd better take me to the hospital."

"Oh, baby, are you sure?" my father asked. They had no insurance, and they'd intended to have a home birth. Over and over he asked her if she was sure she needed to go to the hospital. She did not answer him. She lay in the backseat of the car feeling worse all the time, and my father drove fast, then faster, back toward Tupelo. By the time they got to a hospital, my mother could no longer walk. She was diagnosed immediately—she remembered the doctor taking one look at her and saying, "This woman has polio," and then she was put into an isolation room. When her breathing failed the next day, she was transferred to a larger facility and put into an iron lung. I heard this story several times, and I remember asking once if it wasn't frightening, being put into that contraption. "It was a relief," she said. "It was like being pulled out of a pool where I'd been drowning. I could breathe again. You have no idea what a relief that was. I remember telling myself, *I'm alive. I won't think about anything else now; I'll think about that tomorrow.* Just like Scarlett. I thought that every day for three years until I got to come home."

"You don't think it anymore, though, do you?" I asked her.

She smiled at me.

"Do you?"

"No," she said. "I don't think that anymore." But she was lying. Denial was not a bad thing, in her mind. And I have to say, I think it served her well.

She talked very little about the time she spent in the lung. Over the years, I'd learned bits and pieces of information: that there were many iron lungs, all in one large room, and the only privacy was curtains that were sometimes drawn between them. That her iron lung was a mustard-yellow color and her neighbor's a muddy green. That one Christmas Eve, the patients had sung—with difficulty, of course—"O Holy Night," and it had made the staff cry. That the sound the bellows made with their rhythmic squeaks and thunks reminded my mother of windshield wipers. That when someone died, the patients' overhead mirrors would be turned so that they couldn't see the now silent iron lung being pushed past them. That my mother read three books at a time from her overhead rack so that the page turner wouldn't be needed so often. That the women patients wore their hair in topknots, necessary because of lying flat in the iron lung, and the style was called a "polio poodle." That a psychiatrist once asked my mother, "How does it feel to realize your daughter will never know your touch?" (To which my mother responded, "How does it feel to be an incompetent asshole?") That a patient once complained of feeling cold and his caregiver put a blanket over the lung rather than him. That the patients who couldn't talk made giddyup sounds to call for help, or clicked their teeth together, or made a popping sound with their lips. That there was a ward newspaper to which my mother contributed poems and short stories. She learned, in occupational therapy, to write with a pen held in her mouth; it took an hour and forty-five minutes for her to write one page.

I asked once if people ever cried, and she hesitated, then said yes. "Did you?" I asked, and she said yes, but rarely. And only once had she cried hard and for a long time. It happened after she overheard a conversation between a doctor and a patient a few lungs down from her. The patient, whose name was Sam, asked, "So when will I go home, Doc? I want to drive my new car. Got a new convertible two days before I came in here."

The doctor asked for a chair and pulled it up so Sam could see him, eye to eye. Then he said, "I'm sorry. But I have to tell you that you won't be able to walk again. Or even breathe on your own."

There was a long silence, and then Sam said, "What do you mean?"

The doctor told him again, saying that the time for recovery had passed.

Sam said, "Well, you're wrong. I'll drive to your house. And when I get there, I'll take you out for a ride so fast it'll blow the hair off your head."

"I hope you will," the doctor said. "But Sam, I want you to start thinking about what it will mean if you can't."

It was the night after that incident that my mother had sobbed, at least to the extent that she was able: She said it was more like high-pitched squeals, really, and that that had frustrated her as much as anything, that she couldn't even really have a good cry. But when she had finished crying, she decided that if this was her fate, she would use what she had left. "I could still taste and smell and hear and see," she said. "I could still learn and I could still teach. I could still love and be loved. I had my mind and my spirit. And I had you."

"We have to start charging more than a quarter for our plays," I told Suralee. I had taken her through the hole in the latticework at the side of my front porch for what I considered a staff meeting. We were sitting in the dirt, leaning against the foundation of the house.

"Can't," Suralee said, scratching her arm. She looked around. "I don't think we should sit under here. I think there's chiggers under here."

"Listen," I said. "We don't charge enough! We could charge fifty cents and make so much more money!"

"Nobody's going to pay fifty cents to see us."

"That's not true! I'll bet we could charge a *dollar*! It's live entertainment!"

Suralee looked at me. "How many people came to our last play?"

I shrugged.

"Four? Counting our mothers and Mrs. Gruder?"

"Well, we need to get more people to come, too," I said. "We need to advertise."

Now Suralee's face changed from thinly disguised contempt to interest. "We could," she said. "We could put up signs all over town. I could make a really nice design."

"See?" I said. "And we could charge more!"

"No," Suralee said. "I'll advertise, but if we charge more, nobody will come."

I sighed. "The trouble with you is, you don't dream big enough."

"I dream big," Suralee said.

"Not big enough."

Suralee scratched her arm again. "I'm getting out of here. We can't be under here."

"But I was going to make it nice for us! I thought we could write under here."

"Let's go and get some ice cream." Suralee disappeared through the hole.

I sat still for a moment, unwilling to follow her command. She was always issuing commands, and I was always following them. But then I decided she was probably right. First we needed to get more people to come. Then, gradually, we could charge more. It aggravated me, how slow fame was in coming.

On our walk to town, Suralee told me about two boys she wanted me to meet. They were brothers, aged thirteen and fourteen, sons of a woman with whom her mother worked. Suralee had met them last weekend at an office picnic. They were blond, Suralee said. Baseball players. I imagined myself in a skirt and blouse and necklace, sitting beside one of them. "Did you ever hit a home run?" I might ask. You were supposed to ask them about themselves.

When we got to the drugstore, Suralee and I headed first to the magazine rack stationed at the front. We sat cross-legged before it, facing each other, the better to share things we would find in the magazines, new styles we favored. Ads for things we would admit our desire for only to each other: Wigs. Nair. Frederick's of Hollywood lingerie.

Mrs. Beasley shuffled over to us. "How is your dear mother?" she asked in her thin voice. I was obliged to answer—these were, after all, her magazines and we were in her store. But I wondered what Mrs. Beasley was looking for, asking me this question every time I saw her. Was she waiting for some story of high drama to add interest to her own life? Was she waiting for my mother to die?

Mrs. Beasley wore a cardigan over her shoulders even in this heat, and her sweater guard was decorated with little pearls. She seemed to fear things getting away from her; she wore a chain on her glasses, and the pen at the counter used by people to write checks was chained down, too. Suralee, her back to Mrs. Beasley, rolled her eyes and grimaced, but I smiled pleasantly. "She's fine. She's going to sunbathe today."

"That girl always did love her tan. How's she fixed for baby oil?"

"Okay, I guess. She didn't ask for any."

"Iodine?"

"No, ma'am, we're just here for ice cream cones. Do you have butter pecan today?"

She looked behind her. "I surely do. And I'll come over to the counter and fix y'all's cones in just a minute."

She moved over to Mrs. Quinn, standing with her new baby in the next aisle, and spoke quietly to her. "Well, thank the Lord, that's a relief. Look yonder, you see Clovis Carter heading out of here all shamefaced?"

Suralee and I rose up to look, too. There was a young black man, accompanied by a white man, leaving the store. They stared straight ahead, not ashamed-looking, it seemed to me, but stony-faced.

"What did he do?" Mrs. Quinn asked. She hiked her baby up higher on her shoulder, held him closer.

"Well, I'll tell you," Mrs. Beasley said. "He came in here with that white boy and they sat themselves right down at the lunch counter. Clovis sat *right next* to the widow Henderson, like to give that old woman a heart attack. She left, of course, didn't even finish her pie. And then they just sat there, even when I asked them nice as can be to please leave. My husband came over and told them they could sit there all day but they wouldn't get so much as a nod. Still didn't move. Finally, Sally came out from the kitchen and spoke to them. I think she told Clovis his hanging around would only make trouble for her. Can you imagine, one of his own asking him to leave! Anyway, after almost two hours, well, they're finally gone."

"It's a shame, all these things happening," Mrs. Quinn said. She shook her head and moved down the aisle, and Mrs. Beasley turned her attention to us.

"Look here, now," she said quietly, "the new *Seventeen* just arrived, and I'm going to give y'all a copy. Free of charge."

Suralee turned around quickly to face her.

"You'll have to *share* it," Mrs. Beasley said, looking pointedly at her. "But I've got to ask y'all not to tell my husband I did that. Can you promise me you won't tell?"

Suralee and I nodded together, and with a sarcasm Mrs. Beasley didn't grasp, Suralee crossed her heart. Old Mr. Beasley with his hairy knuckles and pee stains and bent back and stale breath and toilet paper stuck to his face every day from cutting himself shaving! Who cared what he said? But we would honor our promise.

Mrs. Beasley had never given us a magazine before, and it seemed to me that her generosity was in direct proportion to her unease about what had happened with Clovis Carter. But I didn't care—we were getting a new magazine free of charge.

When Shooter began viciously barking outside, we stood and looked out the window. A man we'd never seen before must have tried to pet the dog, and now he was recoiling, hands held up before him, surrender-style. "Whoa! Message received!"

Shooter didn't bite, but he was not friendly. He lived for Suralee, listened to her exclusively and devotedly. She never put him on a leash, and he followed right behind her and waited outside any place she went in—including school—for as long as it took her to come out. He would doze and snap at flies, stare with intense, tight-muscled concentration at things going by that interested him, but he would never move until she told him to. Most people in town knew him, and they also knew to leave him alone.

The man stepped inside the store, took off his black cowboy hat, and headed for the counter. Mrs. Beasley walked quickly toward him, and Suralee and I exchanged glances. He was very handsome—tall, lean, a nice head of black hair styled in a high pompadour. "Elvis!" Suralee and I said together, and then I smacked her, saying, "Jinx; you owe me a Coke," before she could. Not that either of us ever delivered on our debt. Both of us had a great interest in Elvis Presley, Suralee for the more common reasons, me for reasons a little less ordinary.

When my mother was a twenty-year-old student nurse, she had cared for Elvis's mother, Gladys, when Gladys was admitted to the hospital after becoming ill at the Tupelo garment factory where she worked twelve-hour days as a seamstress. Elvis had visited his mother there, and my mother had met him. Gladys had told her son what a sweet girl Paige Dunn was, how much kinder and more intelligent than the other nurses. My mother said she had been a bit tongue-tied in Elvis's presence—unheard of for someone as fearlessly outspoken as she. It had not been because of his great fame, which had yet to happen, but because of his looks and his smoldering sensuality, even at that young age. She told me he had been very much taken with her, too. "He's crazy for black hair," she'd said, "and he loved mine—he

touched it. He himself had blond hair—he dyes it, you know. He couldn't take his eyes off me. And it was more than my hair he liked, too. I'm sure he's never forgotten me. I expect I'll marry him someday."

She told me this for the first time when I was seven years old, and I believed her. For a few years after that, I told everyone who would listen that my father was going to be Elvis Presley. Oftentimes in the evening, after supper, I would sit out on the porch steps waiting for a baby-blue Cadillac to pull up. How sorry he would feel about what had befallen my mother, how tender! He would swoop her up in his arms and put her and all her machinery in the front seat of the car, and I would sit in the back. On the way to his house, we would sing his songs together and he would comment on my mother's and my ability to harmonize. I figured he had enough money that surely he could find a doctor somewhere who could heal her. My bedroom in Elvis's mansion would have my heart's desire, a canopied bed, and I would be lying in it when my mother, able to walk again, would come in and kiss me good night. "He took so long to *come,*" I imagined saying, and I imagined my mother answering me, "Never mind. We're all together, now." Even after I realized she was kidding about marrying him, I still felt as though my mother—and therefore I—had a special bond with him.

"Elvis" asked for Band-Aids, and Mrs. Beasley directed him to the proper aisle. Then she leaned over the counter to call after him, "I'm Opal Beasley."

"Dell Hansen," he said, turning around.

She straightened and stepped back, fingered her top button. "Oh, my goodness, really? *Handsome?* Well, I guess it fits." She tilted her head and smiled at him. Her glasses were all crooked, as if it weren't hopeless enough.

"*Han*sen," he said gently, and turned down the aisle.

She rose up on her toes to follow his progress. "Just a bit farther down, on your left-hand side."

When Dell came back to the counter, he had a high stack of boxes of various-sized Band-Aids.

"My goodness, Mr. Handsome, is there a war on?"

"It's Hansen," he said, and I was struck by the mildness with which he told her his name for the third time. My mother grew impatient if she had to repeat something once.

"Oh, for heaven's sake," Mrs. Beasley said, and began to laugh. "I'm sorry."

"That's all right; it does a man good to have a lady pay him a compliment. 'Specially one as good-looking as you." He turned toward Suralee and me and winked.

Mrs. Beasley pressed her thin lips tightly together, unsuccessfully trying to hold back a smile. "Well, I did have my days," she said. "I surely did."

"These Band-Aids are for the hardware store," Dell said. "We're all out."

"You work at the hardware store?" Mrs. Beasley asked, for which I was grateful. It was where Suralee and I were headed next, and now it would be infinitely more interesting to go there.

"Yes, ma'am," Dell said. "Today's my first day."

"Where are you from?" Mrs. Beasley asked, and he told her Odessa, Texas.

"And what brings you here?" she asked.

"Just here doing a favor," he said. "For a friend."

"I see." Mrs. Beasley handed him his change. "Well, welcome to Tupelo."

He put his hat back on and tipped it. "Thank you kindly." Just before he pushed out the door, he smiled at Suralee and me. His eyes were an arresting light blue. He had one dimple on the left side. Straight white teeth.

"Kill me dead before I die," Suralee said.

I swallowed. "Do you still want ice cream?"

"Are you crazy?"

We always got along this way. We understood each other. We started out the door and Mrs. Beasley said, "Don't you girls want your cones?"

"We'll be back," I told her.

"Your *Seventeen*?" she asked.

Suralee and I looked at each other, and I ran back to the counter. Mrs. Beasley put the magazine in a bag and handed it to me, then put her finger to her lips; her husband was emerging from the back room. I thanked her, then ran outside to join Suralee, who was waiting impatiently.

We quickly crossed the street, Shooter trotting behind us. Debby's Dress Shop was located next to the hardware store, and I saw Mrs. Black, the owner, standing at the window with her arms crossed, watching us. She was probably afraid we were headed her way, coming in to finger the Ship'n Shore blouses we couldn't afford but liked to look at anyway. If we tried something on, she always checked for smells, and made no effort to disguise it. When Suralee told Shooter to lie down beside a parking meter in front of the hardware store rather than the dress shop, Mrs. Black gave a fake-friendly wave. Hating myself, I smiled and waved back. I had to. Debby Black had once donated a set of saucepans to us. Most had scorch marks and one was missing screws at the handle, but LaRue fixed it for us.

Inside the hardware store, Suralee and I saw not Dell but Brooks. He was standing by a display of paint cans near the front of the store, dressed in a short-sleeved white shirt, shiny navy blue pants, and white socks with his black tie shoes. He was talking to an old colored man; they were laughing about something. "*Hey,* Diana!" he said in his overly hearty way. Suralee always said he should do used-car ads. Brooks only jutted his chin at her—he always forgot her name.

"Hey," I said. "This is my friend, Suralee. Remember?"

" 'Course I do. What can I do for y'all?"

I looked around the store as though trying to locate what I needed, when in fact I was looking for Dell. Suralee began moving across the heads of the aisles, doing the same thing.

"My mom needs something," I said, at the same time that Suralee pointed and said, "Right there!"

"Plumbing supplies?" Brooks asked, for that was the aisle Suralee had gone down.

"No, that's for Suralee's mom," I said. "My mom needs you to look at her icebox."

"What's wrong with it?"

"Not keeping things cold."

"Again?" Brooks looked at his watch. "I can't leave right now, but I can come by after dinner. Tell her we'll have a TV date, how's that?"

I shrugged. She wouldn't mind his company, but I would. They would talk in low voices and ignore me. Sometimes my mother winked at Brooks. Once, I'd seen him rub her hand. He'd used only two fingers and had moved them along slowly; it had made the back of my neck cold.

"Tell her I'll be there about seven-thirty, and I'll bring her a Dairy Queen—doesn't she like Dairy Queen milk shakes?"

"Yes, sir."

"Well, I'll bring her one."

"I like them, too," I said. "Especially chocolate."

"Yeah, I believe that's your mother's favorite, too." He turned again to the colored man. "I'll tell you what," he told him. "I 'bout busted a gut, watching old Randy try to throw that ball. Looked like a goddamn girl."

"Like a girl, you say," the colored man said, then laughed, a wheezy sound.

I started for the aisle I'd seen Suralee go down and saw her standing at the end of it. She was talking to Dell, her hands loose at her sides, relaxed as if she'd known him forever. "Here she is," she said when she saw me. Then, when I reached them, "Mr. Dell Hansen, I'd like you to meet Miss Diana Dunn."

". . . Hello," I said dully, studying the floor. I wanted to look into his eyes and say, "Hi!" brightly, but I couldn't. The only time I wasn't shy was when I was in front of an audience. Last year I had run for secretary of the seventh-grade class and had to give a speech in front of the entire student body. I did all right with that but couldn't handle the one-on-one conversations the candidates were supposed to have in the cafeteria during lunch hour. For two weeks before the election, card tables were set up at the front of the room for the people running for office, and everyone but me chatted easily with kids who'd come up to talk or to ask questions. I'd stared into my lap, afraid to eat lunch or talk, and I lost the election, along with a fair amount of weight. "What's the matter with you?" Peacie had scolded one morning at breakfast. "Way you suck up food, you ought to be busting out of your clothes, not drowning in them." Of course, as Suralee not unkindly pointed out, I wouldn't have had a chance to win anyway. She said no one in our school had the vision to see the noses on their face, much less the kind of qualities a good leader needed to possess.

Dell leaned forward to shake my hand. "Diana Dunn. Sounds like a movie star!"

Suralee gasped. "That is *exactly* what I tell her *all the time*!"

Suralee had indeed told me this, though only once. But I had to agree. Sometimes I lay in my bed at night whispering, "And now, *The Ed Sullivan Show* is proud to present . . . Miss Diana Dunn!!" And then I would say to the audience, "Thank you. *Thank* you! Oh, aren't you nice, thank you all!"

"Suralee just invited me to your play," Dell said.

I looked quickly at Suralee. "You know, the one tomorrow night, in your backyard," she said smoothly.

"It costs fifty cents," I said, avoiding eye contact with Suralee.

"Okay if I bring a date?" Dell asked.

"Yes!" we said together. A dollar!

This was it. Things were starting to happen. This was a sign. There was so much for Suralee and me to talk about—most particularly what we were going to do for a play. We always had a few ideas on hand—the latest featured Suralee playing my mother in a garbage-can iron lung—but nothing was ready to present.

"We'd better go," I told Suralee. There were roles to be decided on, costumes to be designed. Refreshments to be begged from my mother and Peacie. Especially from Peacie. We had a watermelon we might be able to use, but then we would have to follow Peacie's rules: Eat the flesh, but! save the juice in a bottle to drink; bake the seeds in lard and salt; use the white rind for preserves; keep the green skin for her to feed to her chickens. She loved her chickens, and she named them, every one. She said they could cure things. If you got a wart, you were supposed to prick it with a needle, rub the blood on a kernel of corn, and then feed the corn to one of her "children"—your wart would disappear. She swore by it. Also she swore by placing slices of raw potato on your forehead and securing them with a blue bandanna to get rid of a headache. "Come *on,*" I told Suralee, pulling her arm.

"I'm coming!" Over her shoulder, she told Dell, "So don't forget. Eight o'clock, tomorrow night. Green Street, about nine blocks from here, the white house with the ramp."

Dell followed us to the door as we were leaving, and when he saw Shooter lying outside, he said, "Is that y'all's dog?"

"He's mine," Suralee said.

"He wouldn't have anything to do with me before. Mind if I try to pet him again?"

"I don't mind. But he will."

"Just a quick try," Dell said. "I like a challenge."

"Your funeral," Suralee said.

Dell followed us outside. Shooter stood at attention when he saw

Suralee, his tail wagging. But when Dell stepped toward him, his tail stopped and the hair between his shoulders stood up. "It's okay," Dell said, and Shooter growled low in his throat.

Dell stood still, his hand outstretched. "I'll let you come to me, then. Now, let's talk about this, man to man. You don't have to put on a show for me. You know you're curious, so why don't you just come on over and have a little sniff?" The dog stood staring, head lowered.

"He won't," Suralee said. But he did. After the briefest hesitation, Shooter walked up to Dell. He wouldn't allow him to pet him—he ducked when Dell tried—but he sniffed Dell's hand thoroughly. Then he attached himself to Suralee's side.

"I have never seen him do that," Suralee said. "Not one time."

I poked her in the ribs—*Let's GO.*

On the way home I told Suralee, "My mom says if a man likes kids and dogs, he's a good man."

Suralee said, "My father liked dogs and kids. So much for that theory, I guess." She picked up a stone and flung it into a field we were passing, watched it land without comment, then resumed walking. "Hey. Guess what. Tomorrow night is a full moon." She affected an English accent. " 'The loveliest faces are to be seen by moonlight, when one sees half with the eye and half with the fancy.' "

"Who said that?" I asked, and she gave her usual response: anonymous.

"The moon . . . brings all things magical," I said in my own English accent, then added shyly, "I said that."

"I thought so," Suralee said, smiling. She touched my hand. "But it's nice. We'll put it in the play."

"The night can be measured," I said, with no accent at all.

Suralee stopped walking. "Who said *that*?"

"My mother. It's true. There's a beginning and an end to the night.

Because of the sphere shape. You measure from where you can see stars to where you no longer can. It's about the size of the Pacific Ocean." Suralee stared at me. "It's true!"

"How does she know?"

I shrugged. "She read it somewhere."

People brought my mother books from the library or from yard or estate sales, and she read them all. She would have someone fold her hands over her vent hose and then pad them with a towel. The book would rest on this padding, and my mother would hold a pencil in her mouth and use the eraser end to turn pages. She read a lot of mysteries and biographies, but mostly she loved science books.

Suralee pulled at her bottom lip, thinking. It was a characteristic I admired and emulated, just as I imitated the way she watched movies: from the corner of her eye, with her head turned slightly away from the screen. Finally, "We might could use that, too," Suralee said.

We walked the rest of the way home in silence, past houses that grew increasingly less cared for, past a field full of butterflies and grasshoppers and sharp-edged weeds sticking out of orange-colored dirt. We walked past two bare-chested little twin girls swinging on a gate, their mother yelling through the window for them to *stop* that. We walked alongside drooping phone wires held up by poles that had ads stapled on them: a lost cat, a church-group concert, an offer to make money by making phone calls from home. Suralee took a tab with a phone number from an ad promising a weight loss of ten pounds in a week. "You don't need to lose weight," I said.

Suralee said, "It's not for me."

It was for her mother, then. Suralee didn't often speak to or of her mother directly. She had other ways.

"You want to go to Glenwood before we go home?" I asked. Sometimes Suralee and I walked up to the cemetery and lay on the graves. We liked to pretend we were letting dead people speak through us. "I was a hardworking man with a talent for whittling," Suralee might say from her grave. "I died in childbirth on a Saturday morning," I might say from mine. I preferred the darker dramas.

"Not today," Suralee said. "Too much to do." She was right. For the amount of money we'd be charging, this needed to be a good play.

Peacie had sugar cookies for us when we got home. The butter was going to go rancid, she said; that was the reason and the only reason. She piled them high on a plate and set them on the kitchen table. "What you don't finish, you wrap up. Ants getting to be the size of elephants around here."

In the living room, my mother sat with her best friend, Brenda, who'd been the witness at my mother's wedding. She and my mother talked frequently on the phone and visited as often as they could, but it was only about three times a year, now that Brenda had moved to Nashville. Every now and then Brenda would surprise my mother and just show up, and then they'd laugh and talk for hours—about men, about hairdos, about children, about old times. Brenda was a terrific dancer, as my mother used to be. Sometimes they watched *American Bandstand* together, and Brenda would dance in front of my mother. I used to worry it would make my mother sad, but it didn't seem to. She would nod, keeping time, and Brenda would shake her hips and shimmy and twirl. One day she'd grabbed Peacie as a partner, and I'd been stunned to see that snarly woman's fancy footwork. I stood at the doorway, watching, and when Peacie was finished dancing, she came to stand before me, all wild-eyed and out of breath. "I guess you done had your eyes opened," she said.

I nodded, not looking at her.

"Didn't know I could dance. You surprised."

Again I'd nodded.

"That's the Jesus truth. It's a wide, wide world. Sooner you lift up your gaze from your own self, sooner you know that."

"Peacie," my mother had said. "Let her be."

It was one of the few times my mother interfered on my behalf, and

I'd been grateful. "Come over here and light me a cigarette," she'd said. I'd snuck a little inhale, and my mother had smiled. But then she'd said, "Don't get started with something you won't be able to do without."

Now Brenda was showing my mother something in a hairstyle magazine. "See? You really should let it get long again, Paige."

"It's too hard to manage," my mother said. "But I do like that style." She saw me then and asked, "Oh, good. Is Brooks coming?"

"After dinner."

She nodded, worried-looking. "It's gotten worse. I don't know if he can fix it this time."

"He's bringing you a milk shake, and he said how about a TV date."

I mumbled this last, and my mother said, "How about a *what*?"

"A TV date," I said.

My mother and Brenda exchanged glances, and then my mother said slowly, "I guess that would be all right." Again they exchanged glances.

Suralee came into the living room. "Hey, Mrs. Dunn," she said. "Hey, Brenda." Brenda allowed no one to call her by her last name. She said it reminded her of being a "Mrs.," something she'd just as soon forget. "Goddamn men," she said. "Only thing they're good for is nothing." But she didn't mean it. She wanted another man. She talked about it all the time.

"How's your mom?" my mother asked Suralee.

"Okay, I guess."

"Well, you tell her again that if she ever wants to visit, just come on by. Anytime."

"Yes, ma'am, I will."

Noreen would not visit, I knew. She was afraid to visit my mother. She had said so the first time my mother had invited her, though not in those words. But I knew. It made me sad; my mother needed friends to come to the house and see her in the way that Brenda did. Apart from sunbathing, she never went out. I was hopeful that Noreen would change her mind. Ironically, she needed friends more than my mother did.

"Can I go over to Suralee's?" I asked.

"Be back by dinner," my mother said, and turned back to the hairstyle magazine. "Pull the sides of my hair back like that and let me see," she told Brenda.

I started out of the room, then turned around and spoke quickly. "Oh, and can we have a play in the backyard tomorrow night with refreshments? Just a play?"

My mother, distracted, said yes, all right. I looked quickly at Suralee, then away. Outside, we'd celebrate our small victory.

When we passed through the kitchen on the way out the back door, Peacie put her hand on her hip and looked from one of us to the other. "What y'all up to?" she asked. "I know for certain you up to something."

"Nothing," we sang out together.

"What's the matter with you?" Suralee said. "You're not even concentrating!"

We were in Suralee's tiny bedroom, sprawled across her pink chenille bedspread, trying to write the play, and I was coming up with exactly nothing. "It's . . . I'm worried about something," I said.

Suralee turned on her back and sighed. "What?"

I picked up her autograph hound, empty of signatures but for my own. I stroked its ears and sighed. "I think Brooks is trying to be my mother's boyfriend."

"Ew," Suralee said. "What do you mean?"

"He acts goofy around her. He touches her sometimes."

Suralee's eyes widened. "Where?"

"When they're watching TV."

"No, I mean where does he touch her?"

"On her hand. And once he put his arm around her. I saw them."

"Did he ever kiss her?"

"No!"

"How do you know?"

I thought about this. It seemed to me that it would be a terrible betrayal, for my mother to do something I didn't know about. Her life was of necessity unnaturally open to me, and I suppose I believed that as it was my duty to bear constant witness to it, it was also my privilege.

"I'll bet he does kiss her," Suralee said, lying back on the bed and tucking her blouse up into the bottom of her bra. "I'll bet he frenches her. I'm sure he does."

"I'm sure he does *not*! I guess I know my own mother better than you!"

"Whoa!" Suralee said. "Touchy!"

I got off her bed and went to stand in front of her vanity table, looked at myself in the mirror. I picked up a new bottle of nail polish. Cutex. "Slightly Peach." I'd wanted that shade, too. I turned to Suralee, holding the bottle of polish up. "Can I?"

She pooched out her lips, sulking, considering. Finally, she said, "Yeah. Want me to do you?"

I came to the edge of the bed and sat down, not looking at her.

"Why are you all mad?" Suralee asked. "Just 'cause I talked about your mom kissing?"

"Can we put on a record?"

Suralee opened her record box, which was decorated with floating notes. " 'Blue Velvet'?"

"Okay."

She put the record on and then came back to sit beside me. She shook the bottle of polish, and I spread my hands out flat on the bed. Suralee bent her head over them and started painting my thumb with slow, careful strokes. "You know, your mom is really pretty, and she's still young. Don't you think she—?"

"Don't," I said.

"Oh, all right." Suralee continued with my nails, then said, "We'd better talk about the plot for the play."

"The one where the mom gets killed in a car accident?" I asked.

Suralee frowned, considering. "No. Too sad. We'll have a lot of people there."

"Not a lot," I said. "Just more than usual. How about the one with the crazy saleslady?"

"No," Suralee said, then raised her head quickly at the sound of her door opening.

"Hey, girls." Noreen stood before us in her stocking feet with her sad eyes and her faded lipstick. "What are y'all doing?"

Suralee wouldn't answer, I knew; she would never answer obvious questions any more than my mother would.

"Painting nails," I said. " 'Slightly Peach.' "

"Oh, that's a nice one," she said. "I just bought her that. I like it so much I might use it myself sometime."

"Do you want to come to our play tomorrow night?" I asked. "It's only twenty-five cents." Suralee stiffened, but I didn't care. I was going to invite everyone. The more people, the more money. I would invite Riley Coombs and LaRue. Peacie, of course, I had to invite Peacie, and if I had to invite Peacie, Suralee had to invite her mother.

"Oh, I don't know," Noreen said. She turned her head away, scratched at the base of her neck, then moved her fingers up to the top of her scalp, scratching mightily. She did this often, attended to herself as a monkey might, oblivious to whoever was before her. Once, I'd seen her sniff under her arms. She picked at her toes when she watched TV.

"A new man will be there," Suralee said in a singsong voice. "And he's handsome as all get-out. He looks like Elvis."

I knew Suralee's attempt to persuade her mother to come was her natural contrariness—if her mother had said she wanted to come, Suralee would have tried to talk her out of it. But I hoped Noreen would come. I had a certain compassion for Suralee's mother, the way she did for mine. If Noreen came, she could feast her eyes on a real man, rather than the sad specimens she sometimes went out with: bald or fat or poorly complexioned men who honked for her at the curb and took her to cheap places for dinner and then somewhere to have sex, according to Suralee. "Your mother told you that?" I'd asked, horrified, when Suralee had shared this information, and she had looked pityingly at me.

"Do you do the laundry in your house?" she'd asked, and I'd said no, Peacie did. "Well," Suralee said. "I do it in this house. And if you do the laundry, you know."

"Know what?" I'd asked. "What do you mean?"

She'd said never mind, another time.

"What new man are you talking about?" Noreen asked, and Suralee looked coyly down at my pinky, where she was carefully applying a second coat of nail polish. It looked good.

"If you come, you'll see," Suralee said.

Her mother laughed. "All right, I'll come. What's the play about?"

"It's a secret," Suralee said, and told her mother to get out and shut the door behind her, we had work to do. Then, while I waved my hands in the air for my nails to dry, Suralee changed the record and we talked about possibilities for characters until we finally had two we both liked. "Will LaRue come?" Suralee asked.

I said I thought he would.

"Do you think he'd be willing to read a few lines, just a few, at the very end?" she asked.

I told her yes.

"Good," she said. "I have an idea for him. Okay, that's the cast. Now we need to finalize the plot, and get our lines memorized." She handed me a tablet and a pencil. "I'll act the whole play out; you write everything down."

I held the pencil just so, and felt inside myself the swell of pride I enjoyed only with Suralee.

At five-thirty, Noreen, wearing a stained pink silk robe, brought us in bean-and-bacon soup, peanut-butter crackers, and cut-up apples on a TV tray. Folded paper napkins, I noticed, decorated with pink roses. Wasteful. "Why don't you call home and tell your people you'll be eating here?" Noreen asked. It was odd, how she referred to Peacie and my mother that way. She didn't approve of either of them for reasons I felt but did not understand.

"Would *you*?" Suralee asked her. "We're busy."

"I don't think I should," Noreen said.

Suralee looked up at her. "Mom. We're *busy* in here."

Her mother gently closed the door. "She'll do it," Suralee said, and she was so confident I believed her.

When I arrived home at nine-thirty, my mother was furious.

"Where were you?" she asked, her voice even lower than usual. She was seated at the kitchen table; behind her, Mrs. Gruder dried the dishes with elaborate care, then noiselessly put them into the cupboard.

"Where's Brooks?" I asked. She wouldn't do much if he was there.

"Brooks has gone home. Answer me. Where were you?"

"What?!" I said. "I was at Suralee's!"

"And how exactly was I supposed to know you were there?"

"Mrs. Halloway called you!"

"Mrs. Halloway did *not* call me."

I sat at the table opposite her. "Well, that's not my fault. She was supposed to!"

"It *was* your fault," my mother said. "You are responsible for you. If someone says they're going to do something for you, it's up to you to make sure they do it. I was worried about you. I had no idea where you were!"

"Well, you'd have to be pretty stupid not to figure it out."

"Give me your finger," my mother said.

I stared at her.

"Give me your finger!"

I put my left pointer up to her mouth, and she bit me. I drew in a quick breath but did not cry out.

"Is the skin broken?" she asked.

I looked. "No."

"Go wash it out anyway."

Mrs. Gruder, her face hanging low in sorrow, moved to help me, and my mother said, "Eleanor, don't help her. Let her do it herself."

Mrs. Gruder watched me as I washed my hands. I knew that she was in awe of the power my mother held over me. Suralee, too. More than once, Suralee had said, "Why do you just let her bite you like that? Why do you put your finger there? What's she going to do if you just walk away?"

"I don't know," I always said. I really didn't. But my mother, who on that sad day in the iron lung had vowed to use whatever power she had left, did exactly that—with a vengeance. She listened more carefully than anyone: to music, to birdsong, to the wind and the rain, but especially to people—she heard not only what they said but what they felt. She could tell when something in the oven was done by the smell alone; from across the room, she could tell which wrapped box under the Christmas tree held dusting powder. She taught me about good food by her varied and dramatic responses to the taste of it. Most amazingly, she transformed the look in her eyes into her entire body. In anger, those eyes were her grabbing you and holding you down, bending your will to her own. Though she could do nothing but stare at me, I feared her, mightily and distinctly. If she had told me to slap my own face, I would have.

"Now go to bed," my mother said, and I did.

In the morning, I awakened full of energy and bolted to my window to check on the weather—cloudless, I was happy to see; we'd have a nice evening. Then, like a soft punch to the stomach, came a familiar realization: My mother would never again be able to do this, fling back the covers and leap out of bed. Go to the window of her own volition. Go *anywhere* of her own volition. Of course I knew this, knew it in my brain, anyway; but I was nonetheless reminded of it in my heart in these unexpected and most random of ways. I can only describe it as the way you touch something bare-handed that you *just took* from the oven. Impossible as it seems, every now and then I would simply forget my mother was paralyzed. I would hold something out to her. Or I would call her to come over and look at something. I would point at my own mouth to indicate that she had a crumb stuck at the side of her own.

She understood this phenomenon; she'd had plenty of experiences with other people having what she called "brain skips." One summer night, when she was sitting outside with my mother, Brenda felt a June bug land on the back of her neck. Brenda was deathly afraid of June bugs. She'd leapt out of her lawn chair and started dancing around and around, shrieking at my mother, "Get it off! Get it off!"

"Yeah, okay, in a minute," my mother had said.

I once asked my mother if she herself ever forgot her circumstances in this way. "I don't forget," she'd said, "but sometimes I have dreams. And then I have to wake up."

"What kind of dreams?" I asked.

She seemed reluctant to answer. But she said, "Well, I dream . . . it's the simplest things, really. I'm waving. I'm hanging out the wash. I'm just walking down the street, and it feels like floating." Then she said, "I don't want to talk about this anymore, Diana."

This morning, my sorrow at my mother's inabilities was tempered by my anger at her for biting me. I'd gotten up twice to assist her in the night, and beyond her telling me what she needed, neither of us had spoken.

"If you up, get on down here," I heard Peacie call.

"I'm *not* up," I yelled, and moved back into my bed.

"Get down here anyway; I need some help with your mother."

I lay still for a moment, full of a flat kind of hate, then started downstairs. When I left here, when I lived on my own, I was not going to have so much as a cactus to take care of.

I found Peacie in the kitchen, washing dishes. I sat at the kitchen table. "Peacie? Can I ask you a question?"

"You just did."

"We're having a play tonight, and I wanted to know if LaRue could be in it. All he has to do is read a couple of lines at the end."

She shut off the water and turned around. "You want LaRue? In your play?"

"Yes."

She considered this for a moment, frowning, which was often Peacie's way of smiling. Then she said, "He'll do it. What time?"

I told her, then said, "But how do you know for sure he'll do it?"

"I know him, that's how. Since you so worried, I'll call later and check with his *agent.* But right now I need you to help me."

My mother was having her hair washed. Peacie always needed help with that; it was a difficult process. My mother would be wheeled into the bathroom and the backrest of her wheelchair lowered flat. Next, Peacie and I would each grab under an arm and pull her up so that her head cleared the chair and was over the toilet bowl. Then, while I held her head over the toilet, Peacie would pour water over her hair and quickly shampoo and rinse it. It's surprising how much a head weighs; you never really think about it. But it becomes heavy when you hold it this way. And heavier still when you don't want to look into the eyes of the person whose head you're holding. At one point my mother said, "Stop, Peacie." And while Peacie held aloft the battered pot we used to pour water, my mother said, "Are we not speaking, Diana?"

I said nothing.

"Diana?"

Reluctantly, I looked at her.

"I want you to snap out of it," she said. "Susan Hogart's coming here today. She called yesterday."

"So? I'll just get sent outside. That's what always happens. She never talks to me."

"She does sometimes. And she might today."

I shifted my shoulders, tightened my grip at the back of my mother's neck.

"Ow," she said, on her next exhalation, and I said nothing. But I relaxed my hands somewhat.

"So can I rely on you?" my mother asked.

"For what?"

"To say the right things?"

I sighed, and Peacie said, "That's 'bout enough of y'all's summit conference. Let me finish now, 'fore we all fall down."

We washed my mother's hair in tense silence. Then we straightened her up, wheeled her out to her bedroom, and while Peacie put her hair up in pin curls, my mother briefed me on what I should tell the social worker. "You're doing fine; you like your caretakers—whatever you do, don't suggest in any way that there's no one here at night."

"Why is that such a big deal? I know how to do everything."

Peacie and my mother looked at each other. Peacie's face was impassive; my mother looked worried.

"Because if you tell, we could get in a lot of trouble. Diana, you're old enough to know this: We're getting money for a nighttime caretaker. But I use it for other things—things for you."

"And for you!" I shot back.

"Yes. That's right. Things for me, too. But the point is, we're cheating the system."

"You have to!" Peacie said.

"We have to," my mother echoed.

Peacie tied a filmy yellow scarf around my mother's pin curls. The long ends fell down on either side of her head. "You look like one of those floppy-eared rabbits," I said, and my mother smiled. But it wasn't true. Even in pin curls, my mother looked lovely.

"You want to sit by the window for a while, Paige?" Peacie asked, and my mother nodded.

"You come with me," Peacie told me. "I need your help out the kitchen."

"I haven't even washed my face!" I said. "I haven't even brushed my teeth!"

"You think I don't know that? Next state over know that!" She walked toward the kitchen and then looked over her shoulder to see if I was coming. "Move your behind!" she said, and I followed her.

In the kitchen, I sat at the table and she put a bowl of Cheerios before me. "Breakfast in bed—almost," she said. I did not smile. She sat opposite me. "Now, tell me true, you nervous about that social worker?"

"No." I picked sleep from one eye irritably.

"Are too. Now, listen, I seen these things plenty of times. You just answer every question real calm. You say Mrs. Gruder and Janice just fine. And you say I'm the best one. Which I am." She eyed my untouched cereal. "And you eat that 'fore it gets soggy. Don't you make me waste food."

I picked up the spoon and had a bite of the cereal. It tasted good with the wild raspberries Peacie had put in it; they grew in her yard. "Why do you think she'll ask me questions? She hardly ever speaks to me."

"You getting older," Peacie said. "That's why. She been asking your mother about you, talking 'bout puberty." She pronounced it "pooberty," like a science teacher of mine had. "She say she want to start talking to you more often. Today might be the day. Now let's us practice."

She stood up and pushed her chair in, affected a high white voice. "So. Diana, dear. How *you* doing?"

"Just great," I said. "Living here in the lap of luxury. Every day is ecstasy."

"Well, I tell you what," Peacie said. "We can finish in a minute, or you can sit in here all day. Makes no never mind to me." She started humming.

"I'm very *well, thank* you!"

"And how your caretakers treat you?" Peacie asked.

"Oh, they're really good," I said. "Especially Peacie, that angel of mercy, that model of perfection." I was impressed with myself. Hanging around with Suralee was doing me good. I spoke above myself in a way I found thrilling.

Peacie went to the icebox and got out eggs, then took a bowl from the cupboard. "Yup, I got all day," she said. "I'm gon' be here anyway."

"Fine!" I said. "But don't make me practice! Just tell me what you want to tell me and let me go!"

Peacie put the bowl down on the counter and came to stand before me. I stared at the little flowers on the waistband of her apron. "Just don't mess up," she said. "That's all. Don't talk 'less you have to. Be polite and make her think everything just fine. You got no idea what could happen if you mess up."

"I won't mess up!" I said. "I'm not stupid!"

"You ain't stupid," she said, "but you act like it sometime anyway."

"Why don't I just not be here?" I said, but just then the doorbell rang.

Peacie raised her eyebrows and pointed at me, her fingers held like a pistol. I had a nearly irresistible impulse to bury my face in her apron and weep. Instead, I said, "O*kay*!" and gobbled the rest of my cereal.

"I'm coming!" Peacie yelled toward the door. Then she whispered to me, "Tell her you like her dress, or whatever she got on. She always like that. Tell her it's her color, whatever color it is." Her mouth smelled of licorice. She chewed anise seeds, carried a supply wrapped in a hankie in her purse. Once I'd eaten some and she'd smelled them on me. "You steal my breathsweet again I whup your hide," she'd said. She hadn't even bothered to look at me, saying this. But I never did take any more after that.

Susan, wearing a plain yellow blouse tucked into a navy blue skirt, penny loafers, and white socks, seated herself heavily on the sofa and pulled papers out of her briefcase. Peacie, my mother, and I were gathered around her. "Nice skirt, Miss Hogart," I said.

She looked up at me. "Thank you, Diana."

"It's your color," I said, and she looked at me, puzzled. Finally, "Thank you," she said. I cast a murderous glance at Peacie, who looked pointedly away.

Susan shuffled through her papers, then smiled at me. "Everything okay?" she asked.

I nodded.

"Enjoying your vacation?"

Again I nodded.

"What kind of things are you up to this summer?"

I shrugged.

Susan waited.

"I've been to some baseball games. And movies. And swimming. I've been over at my friend Suralee's house a lot. We like to draw pictures. I've been to the library almost every day—I believe I'll finish all the Nancy Drews pretty soon!" I kept my lying voice high and sweet. I sat with my knees together, my hands folded in my lap.

Susan looked satisfied, and though I suspected Peacie was just short of rolling her eyes, her face revealed nothing. I knew a lot more than Peacie thought I did. "Suralee and I are doing a play tonight, in the backyard, me and my friend Suralee. We're inviting a lot of people."

My mother looked over at me, surprised, but said nothing.

"Oh!" Susan said. "What play?"

"One we made up. We make them up."

"Isn't that wonderful!" Susan said, and now I did see Peacie rolling her eyes.

"You want to come?" I asked.

"Well . . . how about if I speak to your mother for a while? You go ahead upstairs, Diana. You must be wanting to get dressed and go outdoors."

"Okay," I said. "Nice seeing you." As I walked past Peacie I smirked, but she was again finding something off to her left fascinating.

By the time I dressed and came downstairs, Susan was leaving. I walked out to her car with her. "Your mother's quite a woman," Susan said.

"She shouldn't be so hard on me, though." My finger was hurting. I was feeling spiteful.

"Well," Susan said. "I don't know a child in the world your age who doesn't think that. It's all part of growing up. Don't you think so?"

I looked up at her plain face, her earnest brown eyes. "Yes, ma'am, I guess so."

"You're a sweetheart, Diana. And just as pretty as can be—you look a lot like your mother." She leaned down and hugged me. I kept my bandaged finger behind me.

From the corner of my eye, I saw Peacie at the window, watching. I wouldn't give her the satisfaction of coming back in to tell her what Susan and I had talked about. I ran down the sidewalk toward Suralee's, and jangling around inside me was thrilling information: Susan had said I was pretty.

Noreen was coming down the steps in her usual go-to-work outfit. But she looked better than usual. She wore a nice white blouse that looked brand-new with a black pleated skirt, and her shoes were red patent leather. A scarf at her neck tied the colors all together. "I'll see you tonight!" she said, gaily waving, and clicked her way toward the bus stop. I watched her go, watched her hips swing, watched her readjust the purse strap that kept sliding off her shoulder. She was just a woman who would always look like she had a greasy mouth, even if she didn't. I went in to find Suralee.

Suralee and I personally invited anyone we saw in town—or on the way there—to our play. And anywhere that would let us, we taped one of the flyers she'd made advertising that evening's performance. I was wildly excited at first, for Suralee had decided to use *The Night Can Be Measured* as a title. But I soon became embarrassed about it; the prevailing wisdom seemed to be that it was a silly title, incomprehensible, in fact, as evidenced by reactions like Brooks Robbins's. "What the hell does *that* mean?" he asked. The librarian said nothing, only smiled a deadly smile. Old Mrs. Beasley said, "The night can be . . . what's that? *Measured?* Huh. Y'all sure about that?" The manager at the grocery store said, "What is this, a science play? Or math or something?" As for Debby Black, she said she was "going out for a Coke" when she saw us headed for the dress shop. She hung the BACK IN FIVE! sign up and came out to lock the door. I noted with satisfaction that she had a run starting in the back of her left nylon. When we asked if we could wait for her return and then post our flyer, she fiddled with her pearls and then said, "Well, you know, I don't really do that, put flyers on my window. I think it's tacky." She whispered this last. When Suralee reminded her that she had a flyer for the Presbyterian church pancake breakfast only last week, she put her hand on her hip and said, "Well now, come *on*. That's different." She looked at her watch. "I've got to run. Say hi to your moms. Tell 'em there's a sale coming on those pillbox hats that are exactly like Jackie's but way cheaper." I imagined my mother in her wheelchair, wearing one of those hats. Then I imagined Noreen wearing one. My mother looked better.

"I guess it's too late to change the title," I said, looking down at the flyers I held. The good news—and the bad—was that I had only three flyers left of the twenty Suralee had made.

"It's a beautiful title," Suralee said. "This is just what artists have to contend with all the time, is a bunch of morons who don't get anything. Especially if it's the least bit poetic. They are absolutely allergic to poetry."

"We could cross it out and put in something new," I said. "We'll just backtrack and put in something new."

"I'm not changing a thing," Suralee said. "I'm going home to rest up. I can't give a good performance without a nap. I need a nap and then I need to suck on a lemon for my voice." She stuck one of the flyers in the dress-shop door and started walking rapidly toward home. I followed, more slowly.

"But maybe people won't come if it's a bad title," I called mournfully after her.

Suralee turned around to look at me. "Like they were going to come anyway," she said.

"True." I felt better, though I knew I should have felt worse.

When we passed the baseball field, a game was in progress. Suralee stopped to watch, then pointed to two blond boys sitting beside each other on the bench. "That's them," she said. "Wade and Randy Michaels. Oh la la. Randy's mine; you can have Wade—he's the younger one. I'm going to invite them to my house some Saturday night when my mother's gone."

"Okay," I said, squinting to try to see them better. Lately I'd been thinking I needed glasses, but I didn't want to tell. One, glasses were ugly; two, they were expensive.

"Can you see them?"

". . . Yeah."

"Can you?" Suralee turned to look at me.

"*Pretty* good."

"Well." She turned back toward the game. "Just trust me." The boys leapt up to run outfield, and Suralee tried to catch their attention by waving, but they didn't see her. "Can you kiss good?" she asked me, starting to walk again.

"What?"

"Can you *kiss* good."

"Oh," I said.

We walked a bit more and then she said, "Well, can you?"

"Ashes to ashes, dust to dust, if you don't kiss, your lips will rust." I smiled at her.

She stopped walking. "Diana. Have you or haven't you?"

I said nothing.

"Oh, no. You *haven't*?"

"I haven't exactly had the opportunity!" I was getting mad. For one thing, I was pretty. Susan had said so.

"I'll have to teach you. You can't just go into this blind." Suralee resumed walking, shaking her head.

"Why are you even talking about kissing?" I said. "You just said we were going to *meet* them!"

"What am I going to do with you," Suralee said in her best world-weary voice. I hated when she did this. I always felt like a baby in a ruffled bonnet, my head lolling stupidly, drool hanging like a shiny silver thread.

When we got back to her house, Suralee pulled me into her bedroom and lowered the shades. "Okay," she said. "I only have a little while." She put a pillow between our faces and showed me how to close my eyes and tilt my head, how to put my hands on the guy's shoulders, how to move my head in a kind of circular motion when kissing to make it "sexier." I grew more excited than I wanted her to see; my privates ached. I told her I had to go home, that I'd see her half an hour before the performance, as planned.

When I walked into the kitchen, Peacie said, "Don't sit down, you goin' right back out."

"Why?" Surely I needed to rest, too, though my part was much smaller than Suralee's. She was always the star—and deserved to be, I had to admit.

"I need you go to the store."

I started to protest. When I went for groceries, I had to put the laundry basket in a red wagon and then pull it along behind me. I was too old for that now; it was embarrassing. But Peacie said, " 'Fore you start whining, just listen up. Your mother told me make y'all a sheet cake for tonight. I ain't got enough milk or eggs. Or butter. Considering her kindness in feeding your audience, you'd best *fly* back downtown."

I dragged myself to the door, then turned back. "LaRue has a part in the play, you know."

"I know he do. I'm the one told him, so I guess I know."

I was hoping she'd say he could drive me to the store. That it would occur to her that since he was in the play, he should contribute in some way toward helping provide refreshments for it. But that wasn't going to happen. Peacie stood looking at me, her arms crossed, her eyes narrowed and burning into me. "I'm going!" I said. *"God!"*

"Keep your voice down, your mother napping," Peacie said. "And keep the good Lord out of it."

I stomped off toward town, hoping no one would see me, hoping especially that the boys playing baseball would pay me no mind. I thought of my mother, resting in the dining room, wet sheets hung before the fan to keep her cool. Sometimes she was just like a princess, I thought—there was no difference. Manicures and hairstyling and someone preparing your every meal. Afternoon naps. A *lazy* princess! Then I shrank down small inside myself, seeing that I was capable of such thoughts.

When I got back home, Peacie and my mother were at the kitchen table, cups of coffee before them, my mother's with a straw in it bearing the usual traces of her red lipstick. My mother oftentimes used a straw, as her wheelchair was slightly reclined and it made drinking easier. But I never got used to the sight of a straw in a cup of coffee—odd the way that it, more than anything, said *handicapped* to me.

Peacie was holding the phone up to my mother's ear. "Hold on a minute," my mother said. And then, to me, "Brenda's coming to your play tonight!"

"Really?"

"Really!"

"Is she going to spend the night?"

My mother nodded, smiling.

I loved it when Brenda spent the night. She and my mother would stay up late giggling and gossiping like schoolgirls. Once Brenda had brought along a scrapbook, and they pored over the pictures, reminiscing about this thing or that. I liked to listen to them talk, liked to hear stories about when my mother was normal. There was a picture in that scrapbook of my mother and Brenda out on a double date. They were dressed identically in jeans and short-sleeved sweaters, and they had scarves tied around their necks. They had gone horseback riding, and

Brenda's date had spent the entire time in pursuit of another woman, who was in a riding party just ahead of them. But my mother's date had been a peach. "I wonder what ever happened to him," Brenda said, gazing at his handsome face. He was a curly-headed blond man with an excellent physique.

My mother stared, too, then said wistfully, "Maybe he got polio and he's a quad now."

There was a silence, and then they burst into peals of laughter. I didn't quite understand the humor, but I laughed, too.

"You can always hope," Brenda said, and this set them off again.

I took the phone from my mother's ear and told Brenda I was so glad she was coming.

"You want anything from the city?" she asked, and I said yes, an apartment.

"Maybe next time," Brenda said.

I put away the groceries, then went to my room. I looked in the mirror to check for I never knew what, then flopped down on my bed, looking at our flyer. Suralee had taken one of the last three; I'd put one in Riley Coombs's mailbox and had held on to this last one. Suralee had done a nice job making the printing fancy; it looked to me like something from royalty. A letter from the king. I'd been planning on keeping it, taping it into my scrapbook. But now I got another idea.

I turned the flyer over and began a letter to Elvis Presley. He would miss this performance, but who knew? He might want to come to another one. He might want to come back and visit Tupelo, take a look at his crummy two-room, cold-water frame house just for the good shudder he'd get. And I thought he might like to know some other things, too. *Dear Elvis,* I wrote in my finest hand. Then I erased it and wrote, *Dear Mr. Presley.*

There were often nights when I couldn't sleep well. It had nothing to do with getting up with my mother. Rather it had to do with a kind of anxiety I talked myself into, a kind of downward spiraling familiar to anyone even mildly acquainted with insomnia. It came from too many *what ifs*, too many uneasy projections into the future that could make you feel bitten about the edges. But tonight, many hours after our play, I couldn't sleep for another reason, and that was because of a wild kind of happiness, because of the excitement of believing that Suralee and I were at last on our way toward certain fame. I couldn't wait to tell *Photoplay* that I knew the exact night it had all started.

We'd had what was, for us, a huge audience. Fifteen minutes before the show was to begin, Suralee and I had stood at my bedroom window, watching people come. My mother and Peacie and LaRue, of course. Brenda collected money in a cigar box, and more than once I heard her say loudly, "Tips *are* accepted!"

Noreen Halloway came, wearing false eyelashes and white lipstick and, according to Suralee, perfumed to high heaven with Intimate. Brooks Robbins came with Holt Evers, who worked with him at the hardware store, making good on his promise to bring someone to "beef up the crowd." Most people sat on the ground, on sheets we'd spread over the lawn (with Peacie's reluctant permission). But Opal and Hamilton Beasley sat in the front, in two of the four chairs provided. Another chair was taken by Dell Hansen's date, who turned out to be not a glamorous young woman but rather Rose Trippett. "She must be two hundred years old!" Suralee said. Old Mrs. Trippett was the grandmother of Ben Samson, who'd been almost famous as a football player but had been killed in a freak accident at practice one day—his neck had been broken. The fourth chair stayed empty, as though accommodating a ghost. Suralee said it was good luck in theater, to have one chair empty.

Before we went upstairs, Suralee and I had seen Dell arrive in a brand-new black Pontiac—a GTO, he said. It was a fine car, thrilling, and it looked so strange, parked outside our house. I hoped those neighbors who had declined coming to our show would see it. Not that they would ever admit to me that they had.

Dell looked every bit as good as before, if not better. He was taken aback when he met my mother—his face had colored, in fact, when he first saw her—but he quickly recovered. He leaned down to say nice to meet you. He smiled at her. He touched her hand.

Just before Suralee and I were ready to go down and start the show, Riley Coombs came limping into the backyard. He was dressed up, for Riley. This meant that he had combed his hair and tucked his shirt in and tied his shoes. I couldn't be sure from where I stood, but he even looked clean-shaven. He sat far in the back, putting some distance between himself and the others. He was like an octopus, I thought, scary-looking but really very shy.

We'd laid out four flashlights to be footlights. My mother had agreed to let us put all the house lights on for our performance, and as darkness began falling, they provided a wonderful glow, which is exactly what we'd intended.

When we were ready to begin, I held up a blanket and announced, "*The Night Can Be Measured,* a new play written and performed by Suralee Halloway and Diana Dunn. Tonight's performance is the world premiere."

Behind me, while I spoke these words, Suralee climbed quietly into our garbage-can iron lung, which was lying on its side and decorated with gauges and portals we'd drawn in with black crayon. Suralee's compact served as the overhead mirror. We had cleaned the can with bleach and lined it with newspaper, but it still had a bit of an odor. Suralee had said she'd be so into character she wouldn't even notice. She was wearing all black, something she was otherwise not allowed to do, and her hair was in a high ponytail, tied with white ribbons. The hairstyle was modeled after one we'd seen in a newspaper photo of my mother, just minutes after I was born. In that photo, she lay in the iron lung with her ribbons and her red lipstick, and a nurse held me off to the side and above her. After the photo was taken, my mother had asked the nurse to show her my fingers and my toes, and my mother had counted them aloud. Then she'd asked the nurse to hold my hand to her mouth and she'd kissed me and the nurse had dripped tears onto my head. "Baptized," my mother had said.

Our play centered on a woman in an iron lung whose doctor falls in love with her one moonlit night. Once Suralee was inside the can, I dropped the blanket, went behind the lilac bushes that grew in our backyard, then emerged again, transformed into Dr. Larson. I wore a man's white shirt someone had recently donated to us, cut at the knees to be lab-coat-length. I carried a clipboard. In my front pocket, for lack of better props, were a wrench, a screwdriver, and a pair of scissors. "Well, well," I said to Suralee. "And how are we doing this evening?" I crossed my arms over my chest and stood with my legs wide apart, as I'd been instructed.

"Dr. Larson!" Suralee said, in a voice not quite her own. "What ever are you doing here at this hour?"

I hesitated—grandly, I thought. Then I said, "Well, I . . . I don't quite know. But I do know that the loveliest faces are to be seen by moonlight." I sat on the ground beside her and reached out to touch her face. "For that is the time when one sees half with the eye and half with the fanny. *Fan*cy!"

Suralee grimaced but quickly regained composure. The play went on from there, a conversation between the doctor and the patient that showed how much they had in common, despite their glaring differences. They talked about their favorite season, their favorite songs. Something we'd never quite gotten right in rehearsal worked flawlessly in the play—we said something at the same time, then at the same time said, "Jinx, you owe me a Coke." We gaily laughed and then stopped suddenly, for we realized what we both were feeling. Suralee said, "This can't be happening. It's impossible. It's like trying to measure the night."

"The night can be measured," I said.

Suralee laughed. "No, it can't!"

I told her how—too mechanically, I realized; I was afraid of forgetting the lines.

"Why, that's . . . that's *beautiful,*" Suralee said, and she was so convincing she made up for my wooden presentation. I looked into her face, lowered my voice as much as I could, and said, "Very beautiful." I made sure not to look away too fast, so that the audience would understand that it was she I found beautiful. Then, in a fine, tremulous tone, I admitted my love for her, and asked if it was possible that she could care for me, too. Could she, possibly? Yes, she breathed—we'd written that into the script, *Yes, she breathes*. In that case, I said, would she come to live with me? Again she breathed Yes, oh yes. Then our favorite part, the dramatic pulling back just as Suralee and I were about to kiss because another patient was in trouble and needed me. "Will you wait for me?" I asked, and Suralee said, "I know that the moon brings all things magical, but just where do you think I might go?" This was a tribute to my mother's sense of humor, and I snuck a look to see if she was smiling, which she was. I ran offstage, concern for the next patient evident in my face, my cardboard stethoscope slapping against my chest. I disappeared behind the bushes again, and LaRue stepped forward and turned to face the audience, a piece of paper Suralee had given him in his hand. He cleared his throat, smoothed down his tie. "Love," he began, then stopped, removed his hat, and started again. "Love does not have legs," he slowly read, his finger moving along. "It does not have arms. But it move mountains." He put the paper down at his side, obviously relieved, and Peacie leapt up and began wildly applauding him. The others followed, though I hoped some of their applause was for us, too.

We had cake afterward, Peacie's delicious buttermilk chocolate, and everyone was saying how much they had liked the play, how imaginative we were, what good actresses. When I talked to Dell, he told me that Rose Trippett was his best friend Ben's grandmother. "Ben Samson? That football player?" I asked, and Dell said yes, that in fact he himself had been a football player, too, on the same team as Ben, but had quit after the accident. He'd always promised Ben that he'd come with him to Mississippi to visit Rose sometime—Ben had told Dell how nuts he was about his grandmother—but Dell never had. But now he was staying with Rose for a while, making sure she was all right, and deciding what he wanted to do next with his own life. Noreen stood right next to Dell until he left—early, as it happened, because Rose grew tired. And then Noreen glued herself to Brooks, who was glued to my mother—and she left when he did.

I lay in bed, thinking about Brooks. It might not have been such a good idea to do a play about loving a woman in an iron lung; it might have given him ideas. Not that he didn't seem to already have them. Tonight he had told my mother that he would like to take her out to dinner sometime. My mother had laughed. Out to *dinner*! she'd said. Brooks had said sure, how about it. My mother had said it would be pretty hard with all her equipment—she could frog-breathe long enough to get somewhere close by, but then she'd need to get plugged in again. Brooks had said his friend Holt would come, he would help carry the equipment, and they'd make sure the restaurant had an outlet near their table.

"But you'd have to feed me and everyone would stare," my mother had said, and Brooks had said he would pick a corner table and she would sit with her back to the people. I'd been sure she'd refuse him, but she didn't. "Well, maybe," she'd said, and she was smiling. Dell had overheard this conversation—it took place just as he was getting ready to leave—and had come over to look more closely at my mother's equipment. "Seems like you could hook that one box up to a battery and then build something onto the back of your wheelchair that could carry what you'd need," he'd said. "Just a plywood extension would do it."

I loved that he wasn't afraid of my mother, that he seemed to see past everything and acknowledge her as a person. It was a rare thing. Brooks had gotten all excited and said yes, that was right, he'd thought about that himself, he'd get to work on a design for it at the store tomorrow. "I'll help you," Dell had said, and Brooks smiled uneasily and said okay.

Suralee and I had been watching this, and I'd said, "Ugh! Look at him! See what I mean?" Suralee had said she thought it might be good for my mother to have a boyfriend. "Yeah, if it were someone like Dell," I'd said, and Suralee had said she didn't really think Dell would be interested in my mother. She'd stared straight ahead when she said this, and I'd seen that she wanted Dell for her own mother. *That'll be the day,* I'd thought. Noreen had no more chance than my mother did. At least my mother was pretty. At least she was smart and funny. And Dell had liked her, I could tell. You could tell these things. She'd invited him to come back to visit, and he'd said he would.

I got out of bed to stand at the window and look out at where our play had taken place. I was eager to do another one and make more money, but Suralee said we had to do a different project first, one that could net us far more than our plays did. There was a sweepstakes she'd seen in one of her mother's magazines. All you had to do was collect Sweetnuf cookie and cracker labels and send them in. Send in as many entries as you like; you could win five thousand dollars and a trip to the World's Fair—that was first prize. Twenty-five hundred was second prize, five hundred dollars was third.

There were five days left to enter. We were always entering sweepstakes, and we had never won anything. But I agreed to help her find as many labels as we could. We'd go door-to-door, begging, as usual. Then we'd get started on the next play. It would be about Noreen—she herself had requested that.

I climbed back into bed and lifted up my pajama top so that the fan would blow on my skin. It was so hot and humid. Other kids would be out on the lawns, sleeping on mattresses they'd dragged outside. But I was not like other kids, as my mother was not like other mothers. Forever and ever. This I would tell *Photoplay,* too. To their great admiration, I was sure.

"We plumb out of everything," Peacie said, shaking the nearly empty cereal box. "You didn't get half what I done told you to get last time."

"We didn't have enough food stamps," I said.

"Well, we got more now. I want you go back to the store. And I'm gon' call LaRue help you, make sure you do it right this time."

"Can't," I said. I was at the kitchen table, looking through the *Seventeen* Mrs. Beasley had given us. I had to give it to Suralee later on—my turn was up.

"What do you mean, you cain't?"

I didn't look up. "I made plans with Suralee. We're going to go somewhere. She's coming to get me in half an hour."

"Oh, I see. You just went right ahead, lay out your day, never mind checking with anyone else."

I turned to look at her. "That's right. And I can't go to the store."

"Well, you gon' surprise yourself, because you will."

"Suralee and I are entering a contest, and we need to collect box tops! We need the whole morning to do it!"

Peacie was quiet for a moment, wiping a plate. I knew she was reconsidering. Peacie liked sweepstakes, too. She herself would often enter, though never more than once. She put the plate in the cupboard, then said, "Did I *say* you going to the store this morning? No, I did not. You can collect box tops this morning, but you be back by noon. Or your behind meet up with a certain wooden spoon."

"You can't spank me anymore, Peacie," I said. "I'm too old."

"You too old, you say."

"Yes, I am."

"Well, I'll tell you what. If you so old, you don't need no one beg you to get groceries that is mostly ate by you."

"I said I'd go!"

"That's what I said, too. We in agreement, ain't that something. Now see if your mother done with that bedpan."

I looked out the window on my way to the dining room. Trees moving in the wind. Wide blue sky. Miles of it. Birds soaring obliquely on an updraft.

My mother was done with the bedpan all right. "Get Peacie, honey," she said. "Don't you do this one."

There were these small mercies.

"How are we going to pay for the envelopes and stamps?" I asked Suralee. We were walking home, carrying the amazing number of box tops we'd gotten. It seemed as though everybody liked Sweetnuf brand, and almost no one else was entering the sweepstakes. Suralee said it must not have been advertised in many magazines. In just under four hours, we'd collected 186 box tops—12 of which had come from one house alone.

"I'll get some money from my mom," Suralee said. "You can get it from your mom."

"Right," I said bitterly.

Suralee grabbed at a passing bumblebee. I jumped back, saying, *"Don't!"*

"Relax," she said, and smiled at me sideways, the way she sometimes did.

"One of these days you're going to catch one and get stung," I said. I hoped for it, actually. It seemed she deserved it. I didn't wish her pain, only consequences.

"You need to come up with about ten dollars," she said.

"Ten dollars!"

"We need good envelopes," Suralee said. "Real thick ones that will just leap into someone's hand."

"What if we won first prize?" It hurt my chest to think about it.

"I *know,*" Suralee said.

We silenced ourselves—with our respective visions, I was sure. In mine, my mother's caretakers were white registered nurses. They wore white uniforms and white nylons and caps. And they were there all the time, day and night. All night. I had my canopied bed, I had a wardrobe full of clothes, and I went to a fancy school. Not in Tupelo.

When Suralee and I got to my house, we saw Dell's car pulled up in front. We looked at each other, understanding immediately what we needed to do. We tiptoed up onto the porch and looked in the front-room window. No sign of anyone. Then we heard voices coming from the backyard, so we crept alongside the house, behind the bushes, until we could see Dell sitting on the ground beside my mother. Peacie was a distance away, hanging sheets on the line. My mother was in her turquoise bathing suit, her back to us.

Suralee pointed toward the upstairs of the house. She meant that we should go into my bedroom, which was directly above my mother, so that we could hear their conversation better. "The screen door's locked," I whispered. Suralee rolled her eyes. She motioned for me to follow her, and we went back to the front-porch door.

"Now watch," Suralee said. She pulled the screen door outward the short distance it would go, slid a box top into the small crack, and then quickly jerked it up, lifting the latch. We went inside and locked the door behind us, then raced up to my room.

We sat cross-legged, directly beneath my window. Suralee closed her eyes to hear better; I pressed my hand over my mouth and stared hard off to the side, my own way of concentrating. "No reason it won't work," Dell was saying. "Couldn't be easier. After I bring Brooks back the measurements, he'll finish building the platform today. I'll give him a hand attaching it."

"I can't believe I'll be able to go out, just like that," my mother said. "And to a restaurant!"

"Are you nervous about it?" Dell asked, and I liked it, the ease with which he asked this rather personal question.

"I guess I am," my mother said, laughing a little. "I know everyone will be gawking at me. But you know, I *should* go out once in a while."

" 'Course you should," Dell said, then added, "Hell, I'll take you somewhere. You want to go somewhere with me sometime?"

There was a thrilling pause. I looked over at Suralee, but she wouldn't open her eyes. Then I heard my mother say, "Of course I want to." And this I did not like. There was a tone I did not recognize in my mother's voice. Things were all of a sudden moving too quickly for my taste. And too oddly. My mother, going out, with a man. With two!

Suralee stood up. "I gotta go."

"What's the matter?"

"Nothing." Suralee pulled the box tops from the waistband of her shorts, made two even piles, and handed me one. "Mail these tomorrow," she said. "Buy envelopes and stamps and mail them. Be sure you enter in your mother's name—you're not old enough to win."

"I thought we were going to address them together!"

"No."

"But you said—"

"I changed my mind. We have to do it separate. One of us might win, and . . . there can't be any confusion!"

". . . Okay." My arm itched, but I wouldn't scratch it until she left. It was bad enough she was standing above me, looking down at me.

"Remember, mail them tomorrow!"

"I *will*!" I watched her go. You could not reach her when she got like this. It had happened before that she would suddenly turn moody and pull away. She assigned herself certain privileges for being an actress in the making, and I believed she was entitled to them. Anyway, I wanted to listen to my mother and Dell without her. I wanted the space to feel whatever I felt, to not worry about what showed on my face. I waited for a minute, then went downstairs to lock the screen door again.

Back up in my room, I leaned on the windowsill and chanced a peek into the yard. Dell was looking up at my mother, and I feared he'd see me, so I quickly lowered myself back down to a sitting position. I could hear them well enough, and I'd seen what I wanted to: Dell's handsome face, open and accepting, looking at my mother like he was just a man and she was just a woman. My mother had a widow's peak, which gave her face its lovely heart shape, and she had a dimple in her chin. In strong sun, her black hair gave off blue highlights. She wore perfume; she had Peacie put it on her every day. Was he noticing all this? I wasn't sure if I wanted him to or not. In my stomach was a knotted-up feeling. I could feel my heart beating in my ears.

"I don't know where your daughter got to," I heard Peacie say. "LaRue be here soon, and I *told* her she got to go the store with him."

I bolted downstairs, raced out the front door, and walked around to the backyard. I'd need to get inside before anyone else so that I could lock the screen door again. If Dell wasn't there, I'd have run right in, saying I had to pee. As it was, I greeted him casually, then walked slowly to the back door. "Hold up," Peacie said. "I want you to take this laundry basket down the basement."

I hesitated, then took the basket. Peacie followed me into the house. If she went into the living room, she'd see the open front door and start asking questions. I put the basket down just inside the back door and ran ahead of her. "Where you going?" she called after me. "I told you take this basket downstairs."

"I think LaRue is here," I said. "I heard a horn. I'm just going to tell him I'll be right there."

I ran to the screen door, pushed it open and looked outside, then came back in. "Nope," I said. "It wasn't him." I put the latch in place, then walked past Peacie—with her crossed arms and narrowed eyes—to get the laundry basket.

"You hiding something," Peacie said. "What you hiding?" She swatted at a fly buzzing around her. I didn't answer. "Listen here," she said. "After you take that laundry basket down, get the swatter and send that fly to glory. And when you go with LaRue, I want you mail them bills on the kitchen table. Count them, and that's exactly how many I want you have in your hand 'fore you put them the box."

Peacie did this every time I mailed something—told me that I should count the envelopes when I first picked them up and then again before I dropped them into the mailbox. If I did not have the right number, I was to bring them all home so she could see what I'd lost. I had never lost anything, but she always told me to count.

Today there were five envelopes: the electric bill, the phone bill, the rent, the Sears bill, and one more, a plain envelope with money being sent to the Red Cross. My mother never had money to spare but gave to a charity every month anyway. She put no return address on the envelope, and she sent cash—it was important to her to make her donations anonymously. I thought for her to give away money was insane, and I told her so on a regular basis. "It's very little that I send," she always answered. And then she always added, "You'll grow into an understanding of why I do it." I was sure I would not. For one thing, I didn't want to understand. I wanted the money.

There was a hole in the floor of LaRue's car. I liked riding with him for that reason, the sight of the black road rushing by below us, the safety of me sitting above, incapable of ever falling through that four-inch hole—but what a thrill to imagine it!

"How you doing this fine afternoon?" LaRue asked as we pulled away from the curb.

"Okay," I said. He was wearing a new hat today, and I complimented him on it.

He thanked me, then said, "Now I'm gon' show you something make your eyeballs spin in they socket."

"What?"

Without taking his eyes from the road, LaRue took off his hat and showed me the inside. There was silk lining, all in rainbow colors. He snuck a look at me. "Ain't that something?"

"Yes, but my eyeballs aren't spinning."

"I bet your heart be lifted up, though. Ain't it?"

I smiled. "I guess so."

"Well," he said, putting his hat back on carefully, just right. "That's even better." His voice was so warm and slow, I liked him so much. I couldn't imagine what he saw in Peacie. Today I decided to ask him.

"LaRue? How come you love Peacie?"

He laughed, then bent his head sideways to have a good look at me. Handsome, too, LaRue was. "What you mean? Don't you love her, too?"

I said nothing, stared tactfully straight ahead.

"Well, I think she a beautiful woman. She got those big eyes, those cute little ears. Mostly she got a big heart. She a *good* woman."

"Peacie?" I couldn't help myself; it burst out of me like spurting liquid when you've just taken a drink and someone makes you laugh.

He laughed again. "I know you think she mean. But she ain't in her heart, that's where the difference lie. Some people act all nice on the outside and they got a heart like a dried-up prune. Peacie the other way around. And you know, she love you like her own child."

Now it was my turn to laugh.

"You growin' up fast, Diana. When you growed up some more, you understand."

Somewhere inside me, I thought he was probably right. Nonetheless, I straightened in my seat, looking to reclaim some sense of outrage, to continue my move from fear of Peacie into a kind of equality with her. I had felt the budding of such independence just this morning, when I told her she could no longer spank me.

What came to me now, though, was a time I was eight years old and found a kitten in the backyard, on Christmas Day. It was a dirty little calico, shivering and mewing, sneezing a little, and so thin you could feel every bone. I brought it inside and asked my mother if I could keep it. No, she said immediately. I began to cry, saying the cat would die if we didn't take it in. My mother said it wouldn't; it would find another home or fend for itself, but we couldn't have it, we couldn't afford it. There would be vet bills and cat food, litter and a cat box—we couldn't afford it. I put the cat back out and it ran away, which hurt me even more—had it not understood my intentions? Couldn't it at least have hung around in the yard and let me keep it that way? I would have snuck scraps out. I would have brushed it every day. Callie, I would have called it, and I would have found blue ribbon for its neck.

The next morning Peacie had come into my bedroom with a small wicker basket holding a stuffed animal cat and her three kittens. "What's this?" I'd asked, and she'd said, "Some foolishness somebody give me that I do not want. You can have it." I stared at the basket but did not reach out for it. Peacie put it on my bed and walked out of the room. I never did thank her for it, and I knew full well that no one had given it to her—she'd bought it for me. I still had it, buried somewhere in my closet. I had never told my mother; I didn't want Peacie to get the credit. Peacie had not told her, either; she didn't want my mother to feel bad for not being able to buy me such things. When Peacie once caught me brushing the little kittens, I'd said I was getting them ready to give them away. "Best brush the rats' nests out your own hair, you be late for school," she'd said. I'd felt bad—I could see that she was hurt.

"Just kidding," I'd said. "I'm keeping them."

"I know that," she'd said. "Fool."

LaRue pulled into a parking place and pointed to a mailbox at the end of the block. "You go mail the bills," he said. "I'll start loading the cart—we got a lot of things to buy. I be in aisle one."

I went to the mailbox and dutifully counted the letters. Five of five. Then, just as I was ready to drop them in, I pulled out the Red Cross envelope and held it up to the light. Ten dollars.

It was a sign. Of course I was meant to take it. I dropped the other envelopes into the mailbox and shoved the Red Cross envelope into my pants pocket. Later I would walk to town and buy envelopes and stamps. I would sit at the picnic table near the ball field and address every one.

LaRue and I filled a grocery cart high with supplies. Large jars of peanut butter and grape jelly, boxes of macaroni and egg noodles, cans of vegetables, big packages of baloney and American cheese. Detergent and dish soap and scouring pads and rubbing alcohol. Potato chips, but not Lay's, we never got to have Lay's, we always had to have the crummy kind that did not have enough salt or crunch. Two loaves of white bread, a dozen eggs. Cereal. Packages of hamburger and chicken wings. Garlic—my mother loved garlic bread with spaghetti. White sugar and brown sugar. Margarine and lard. I watched the cashier ring up the purchases, and so did LaRue—once he'd caught an error, and I don't know who was more proud, me or him.

On the way home, I asked if he was taking a trip.

"Who told you that?" he asked.

"I don't remember. But are you?"

His face grew serious. "Yes," he said. "I am."

"Where to?"

He thought for a while, so long, in fact, that I repeated the question.

"Do you know what this summer is?" he asked finally.

"Nineteen sixty-four?"

"Yes," he said. "It's 1964, and it's Freedom Summer."

"What do you mean?" I was impatient for him to tell me where he was going. It wouldn't be for long, because he never left Peacie for long. But it might be to somewhere exciting. New Orleans, perhaps. The Negroes liked New Orleans. It was full of music and booze—they liked that.

"We got a lot of things going on this summer in Mississippi," LaRue said. "We got a lot of people coming from up north, lot of 'em college students, trying to help the Negro vote."

I thought of the white man I'd seen with Clovis in the drugstore. But they weren't trying to vote. That was something else.

"They got CORE and NAACP and SNCC," LaRue was saying. "A man get confused trying to remember what all those letters stand for. But don't matter what the letters is, I know they trying to change things 'round here should of got changed long time ago. *Long* time ago. So I'm going back home to Meridian, help get folks registered. You remember my nephew, Li'l Bit? I'm gon' work with him."

I was disappointed. This was his trip? Even I'd been to Meridian, on a bus trip with my school choir to sing at another school. Nothing I saw there was exciting. Nothing.

"Li'l Bit got beat up last week. Got his jaw cracked, got a black eye, swelled plumb shut for a couple of days. And he ain't see good before that! But he just keep on. I'm gon' down walk beside him."

"Why'd he get beat up?"

LaRue looked over at me, a rare sadness in his eyes. Then he turned back to the road. "You ever learn something in school, make you want to jump up?"

"No," I answered truthfully. Mostly at school I only looked out the window.

"Well, I done had that happen," he said. "I learn something make me want to jump up. Li'l Bit say the black man won the right to vote in 1868. Now, that's a long time ago! But here in Mississippi, the Negro don't hardly never vote."

"Why not?" I asked. "You just go to the school and wait in line; they'll help you." I had seen this, at my own elementary school. Lines of people, waiting to vote.

"You ever seen Negroes voting?" LaRue asked. I had not. But then, I didn't live in their neighborhood.

"Whole lot of hate in the world," LaRue said. "Whole lot of people don't want the Negro move up from down. When the Negro try to vote, the white man play tricks on him. Tax him. Give him a test he cain't nohow pass, ax him how many jelly beans in the jar. Or tell him he got to memorize a passage from the Mississippi Constitution, and if he mispronounce a word, reciting back? Cain't vote. If he give his age in years instead of year-month-date? Cain't vote. Underline an answer 'stead of circle it, forget to dot an *i*? That's it, cain't vote."

He shook his head. "They send us off to the wrong polling place all day long till it too late to vote. We go to register, they say they run out of applications. They try to scare us, tell us our name be published in the paper, and don't nobody want their name in the paper on account of they gets fired from they jobs. People been arrested, waiting in line to register!

"But this the summer we trying to change all that. President of the United States got his eye on us, seen Li'l Bit in a movie, all the marchers holding they signs say, 'Why Not Help Mississippi Negroes Get the Vote?' Say, 'Integration Is the Law!' They be clapping their hands and singing smack in front of *everyone*! Lord!" He laughed, and in it I heard a frightened joy.

"Li'l Bit teaching in a Freedom School, teach the children a new way to think. Whole new way to look at they own selves, make 'em feel they got the right to stand *up*. He got a friend got him started in all this, but James done disappear, 'longside two white boys. Don't nobody know where they is, but plenty of us thinking they dead. The Klan be burning churches, they be firebombing houses, they be beating up people want to help. They be lynching." He looked over at me quickly. "Best not say I told you that. I'm a fool, tell you that. Your mama like to keep you innocent."

"It's okay," I said. "I won't tell." I was beginning to feel odd inside. Why would this be happening? Who cared if Negroes voted? Who cared if anyone voted?

"You know, it was Li'l Bit taught me to read," LaRue said.

I looked over at him and saw tears in his eyes. "I know," I said. I reached over and touched his arm lightly. "You read good, LaRue."

"Thank you." He wiped at his nose. "I'm gon' help out," he said. "I got to do it. I'm glad to."

We said nothing for a long time. And then I said, "LaRue? Can I open the chips and have one?"

"I 'spect you can."

"I'm not supposed to."

"I know that. But I 'spect you can anyway."

I reached behind me for the bag with the chips on top. "You want one?"

"I believe I will."

We crunched together, serious and silent. I said only one more thing on the way home. I said, "You be careful now, LaRue."

He smiled at me. "Little mama," he said.

About a week later, when I brought in the mail I found a large envelope for me. My name and address were typewritten. At first I thought it was some sort of report from school, arriving, oddly, in July; then I saw Elvis Presley's name on the return address. I stood stock-still, afraid to open it. But then, my heart racing, I got a knife to carefully split the seam, and pulled out two pieces of paper. The one on top was a large photo of Elvis smiling that Elvis smile, his hair falling in his face. His arm was resting casually on his upraised knee. There was an autograph in one corner, probably fake, but who cared when I had an actual letter from him? When I began to eagerly read it, though, I saw that it was not from him at all. It was only from a secretary, who said thanks so much for writing, all fan letters were passed on to Mr. Presley, and she was sure he would enjoy mine. *Right.*

I went upstairs to my bedroom. I tossed the letter in my trash can, put Elvis's picture at the bottom of my underwear drawer. Then I stretched out on my bed to have a think. LaRue had been gone for a few days, and I kept imagining Li'l Bit all beat up. I saw his hand resting alongside his jaw, his fingers pressing gingerly on his swollen eye. What had he been doing? He must have been doing something; surely no one had beat him up like that for no reason. He must have gone too far.

All my life I had grown up with Negroes close by, yet distant from me. They had their place and we had ours. If everyone held to a certain model of behavior, there would be no problems. White or black, you had to abide by rules set in place long ago, and not cross any lines. Brooks's friend Holt took exception to the friendly ways Brooks had with his Negro customers. I'd once heard him say, "I tell you what, a nigger fuck with me, I be on him like white on rice. You got to keep a boot on their neck, or you end up having to put their ass in a sling." Brooks had laughed and said, "Aw, they're all right," and then he'd looked at the floor, embarrassed, like he'd been called into the principal's office.

I'd also heard, many times, "Educate the nigger and you get a spoiled field hand and an insolent cook." I'd heard it and never thought about it. But only last week I'd heard my mother and Brooks talking about that very thing. My mother said, "If you don't educate someone, they don't have skills. If they don't have skills, they can't get a job. If they can't get a job, they're poor and on welfare. You can't keep someone from being educated, and then condemn them for taking welfare." Brooks said, "I know, but this is too *much,* Paige. They're going too far now." I'd walked into the room and said, "What's too much?" and they'd changed the subject. They must have been talking about the same thing LaRue was, this "Freedom Summer." How far *were* the Negroes supposed to go? Close as my mother and I were to Peacie, there was a separateness enforced by her as much as us.

But now I thought of her standing below me in the kitchen, keeping my mother alive. I thought of LaRue, and I realized I loved him and that my mother loved Peacie, they loved each other. I got off my bed and went over to the window. The clouds were ill-formed today, indistinct. I liked the cumulous clouds better; they looked like clouds were supposed to look.

It made me nervous to think about things changing so much, about college students from up north coming down here to tell us what to do. Everybody watching. The coloreds liked their separateness, didn't they? Everybody was more comfortable with their own! The people in Shakerag didn't want to live with us any more than we wanted to live with them. Those kids from up north had started big trouble and LaRue's nephew had to pay for it.

I moved back to my bed, lay down, and closed my eyes. It was too hard to try to think of what was right and wrong in the world. I wanted to think only about my mother, who was undergoing big changes of her own. She had a date tonight.

It was a date with Brooks, about which she was excited, and she had carefully planned what to wear. Not her normal britches, with the zipper in the crotch that Peacie had put in so that we could put the urinal right up to her—no need to pull down pants and fool around with all that lifting and pulling. Unzip, pee, wipe, zip up, done. Easy. "This is ingenious," my mother had told Peacie when she thought of it. "You should patent this!"

"I 'spect I should," Peacie had said. "I 'spect I should patent my brain; I got a lot of ideas." It came to me now as a warm flush over my chest that when she said that, I was thinking they were Negro ideas. But they were just ideas, free-floating and of no color at all.

But tonight: no slacks for my mother—all of hers had been unfashionable even new, but now every pair was stretched out at the waist and unevenly faded. Tonight she was going to be careful not to drink much of anything, so she wouldn't have to pee. And she was going to wear a dress, a yellow sleeveless dress she had hanging in her closet that came with a matching yellow sweater that had daisies embroidered on it, rhinestones for the centers. She would wear nylon stockings and little yellow heels. I swallowed hard against a lump that formed in my throat. Because I had seen her in yellow, and I knew she would look so pretty and for what.

Peacie stayed late to help get my mother ready. Mrs. Gruder stood by, ready to assist, and I sat at my mother's feet, watching. Peacie applied mascara to my mother's lashes with painstaking care; they were longer than ever. She used lipstick for blush. She made sure my mother's nails were perfectly painted in the rose color they both liked best. When she finished, my mother asked Mrs. Gruder, "How do I look?"

"Like the Breck girl," Mrs. Gruder said, standing before her in plain admiration, her hands clasped.

"Well," my mother said, smiling, "maybe a little."

Peacie also supervised my mother being loaded into Brooks's car. She was like one of her own chickens, running around and pecking at the men, telling them what to do and what not to.

First, my mother was transferred from her wheelchair into the car seat—that was awkward. I stood by, watching helplessly until her dress rose up too high; then I had a job of pulling it down. Next, her wheelchair was put into the trunk, which, thankfully, was large enough to accommodate its high back and new plywood platform. Then Holt climbed into the backseat with the portable respirator, the battery, and the backup respirator.

"Get to that restaurant *soon,*" Peacie admonished Brooks. "But don't go too fast. Don't get in no accident!" Holt leaned his head out the window and said, "Sooner you stop flapping your jaws, sooner we be on our way." My mother looked relaxed; but I always worried when she was frog-breathing that she would suddenly be unable to go on. It was a disconcerting thing, to know that what kept her alive was behind her, and that Holt would have to be the one to act first in case of an emergency.

When the car drove slowly away, Peacie stood on the porch with her hands on her hips. I couldn't tell exactly what she was thinking. I suspected she was caught between two feelings, as I was: It was good for my mother to go out like a real person; it was terrifying to think of the things that could go wrong in the restaurant. Brooks had been around my mother often enough to know how to feed her, how to lift her, the basic operation of her respirator. But what if she did have to pee? What if she choked? What if her equipment malfunctioned? After the car disappeared, Peacie stomped past me to go into the house for her purse. She came back out and walked past Mrs. Gruder and me without saying a word. In her clenched jaw, I saw her worry that my mother, who had already been hurt so much, might now suffer more. Why not just leave things as they were? Why push for a life beyond what she was used to, that, despite its limitations, was at least safe?

"That was her wedding dress," Mrs. Gruder said from behind me. "Did you know that?"

I turned around. "No. I didn't know."

"Well, it was. She told me once. She's kept it all this time. She looks awful pretty in it, doesn't she?"

I nodded. My heart hung heavy and raw-feeling inside me. I wondered what my father had looked like that day, how he had felt, marrying the lively and beautiful girl who was my mother. I wondered what his life was like now. Did he ever think of us? I wanted to hate him, but I couldn't; I didn't know him well enough. Instead, I wondered about him occasionally, with a confused kind of longing. There was a place inside me carved out for him; I didn't want it to be there, but it was. Once, at the hardware store, Brooks had shown me how to use a drill. I'd made a tiny hole that went deep. The place for my father was like that.

Brooks had been pretty fancied-up himself, wearing what looked to be a new shirt and pants, his hair slicked back. He'd brought my mother a wrist corsage of white carnations and a box of Whitman's chocolates, and I was dying to take off the cellophane and the red bow. To have the whole array of chocolates before you, to be the one to get to choose before anyone! My mother had told me I could go ahead and open the box and have some, but I knew enough not to take her up on her offer. It would be wrong.

But now after Mrs. Gruder and I went inside and she disappeared into the kitchen to clean, I removed the outer wrapping, put my nose to the box, and breathed in deeply. The smell alone was delicious. I shook the box and heard the little pleated papers rustling around inside. I lifted the lid and admired the pastel-colored Jordan almonds, the caramels with their little curly designs. The rounded tops of the chocolate-covered cherries—those were my mother's favorites.

I carried the box around and tried it out on different surfaces. The coffee table in the living room, that's where it would be best, I decided. In the daytime. At night I would move it to her bedside. I put it there now, opened the lid, and slanted the box at a tantalizing angle. My mother would probably eat one chocolate a day; last time she'd gotten a box of candy—from Brenda, who sent it to her at Christmastime—she'd done that. But surely she wouldn't be able to eat all of it. I hoped for the Messenger Boy. He was the biggest piece, solid chocolate, and occupied a place of distinction—the very center of the box.

After Mrs. Gruder cleaned up the kitchen, she came to sit in the living room with me. There was something about the evening that became suddenly unbearable to me; I asked if I could go to Suralee's. I saw a quick flash of something in Mrs. Gruder's face—I thought maybe she was hurt that I didn't want to be with her. But to stay there would be like having to disrobe in daylight, like at the doctor's office. To imagine my mother in a restaurant, looking so nice and being stared at so mean, thrilled and killed me; I needed my friend.

"What are *you* doing here?" Suralee asked when she answered the door. I hadn't called first; I'd figured that if Suralee wasn't home, I'd go under my own front porch for a while. Now here was this strange situation: Suralee was home, but she was not glad to see me.

I shrugged. "I just came over."

She poked her head out the door to look up and down the street. Then, "Come in," she said. "Hurry up. I have something to tell you." She was dressed in a skirt and blouse, and the scarf her mother had worn the other day was tied around her neck. She wore her mother's lipstick and eye shadow and charm bracelet, too.

"I have something to tell you, too," I said. I wanted to tell her all about my mother, but I knew I'd have to wait. Suralee had many qualities I admired; patience was not one of them.

"Those boys are coming over!" Suralee said.

"I thought you said tomorrow!" Here I was, dressed in donated mustard-yellow pedal pushers and a pink sleeveless blouse with a spaghetti-sauce stain.

"They *are* coming tomorrow. But they're coming tonight, too."

"So . . . should I leave?"

She looked me over, then said, "No. But let's change you into something else. You can wear my blue dress, only don't spill!"

I followed her to her bedroom. "What are we eating?"

She turned around to look at me. "Drinking. *Booze.*"

I stood still. "What do you mean?"

"Booze! Liquor! I'm going to make rum and Cokes!" She went to her closet and pulled out her blue dress, laid it across her bed. She was nice to let me use it; it was new, and it was very pretty. It would be a bit big for me, but it would still look good. I stood staring at it.

"Hurry up!" Suralee said. "They'll be here any minute!"

"Maybe . . ." I said.

"What? Maybe *what*?" The doorbell rang, and Suralee gasped and covered her mouth. Then she moved to her dresser mirror for a quick look at herself. She pushed at one side of her hair, smoothed the front of her skirt. "Hurry and get dressed," she said. "I'll keep them busy." She started out of the room and then turned back to me. "I'm glad you're here. What would I have done with two of them?"

For the first time, Suralee's acting talent failed her. I knew she would have been just fine with both of the boys. She would have preferred it. I wondered if she had done this before.

I stood still in Suralee's bedroom, listening to her welcoming the boys, telling them that she had a surprise for them. I looked at the dress again, weighed my options, then took off my pedal pushers and blouse.

"You've got to get out of here!" Suralee said. It was almost two hours later, and I lay ill on her bed. I'd thrown up, which made me feel somewhat better, but the room still spun. "My mother will be coming home soon," she said.

"She knows me," I said. Only I said *noash.* I began to laugh. "It's okay if I'm here." My words were lazy and slow.

Suralee came over and grabbed my arm. "Get up," she said. "Oh, I knew I shouldn't have let you stay!" She began undoing the zipper to her dress and caught my flesh in it.

"Ow!" I yelled, from both the physical injury and the pain of her words.

"Shhhh!" She got the zipper undone and pulled the dress down. "Step out of this."

I did, with some difficulty. I was never going to see Suralee again. "I'm not coming tomorrow," I said. *So there.*

"No kidding," Suralee muttered.

"What," I said. "You invited me!"

Suralee threw my pedal pushers and blouse at me. "I'm not even going to talk to you about this! You are drunk!"

"Ha!" I said.

"You need to go home. And of course we're not doing anything tomorrow—they don't even like you. Now get dressed!"

I started to cry. "Why are you being like this?"

She softened, just the slightest bit. "Diana. I have to get you out of here or we'll both be in a whole lot of trouble. We all will. Go home. We'll talk tomorrow; I'll call you as soon as I get up."

I raised a leg to put on my pedal pushers and fell down. "Whoopsh," I said, and started laughing again, though I also felt an enormous sadness expanding within. The boy I'd let touch me in both places already didn't like me anymore.

Suralee knelt beside me and helped me get dressed. Then she walked me to the door and pushed me outside. "Go!" she whispered. "And when you get home, don't talk to anyone! Just go right to bed!"

"Aye, aye, captain," I said, walking backward. I saluted smartly, then turned around and wove my way down the sidewalk toward home.

By the time I got there, the night air had sobered me up a bit. My mother wouldn't be home for an hour; she'd told me she'd be back at nine-thirty. That way Mrs. Gruder would have enough time to get her ready for bed and not have to stay late. I'd be able to speak a few words to Mrs. Gruder and go to bed—she wouldn't suspect a thing. She was dense that way.

My mother, however, was not dense that way. And she was home. As soon as I walked in the door I heard, "Diana?"

I drew in a breath and willed myself to be normal, then went into the dining room, where I leaned against the wall. "Hi," I said. Well done. Just a normal hi.

"Where have you been?" she asked, and I saw that I had not fooled her at all.

Mrs. Gruder was straightening bottles of pills on the nightstand, and I saw my mother's bare shoulders rising above the clean sheet laid over her—she slept nude to avoid the problems caused by wrinkled pajamas pressing into her skin. The large sheepskin she rested against at night had been placed behind her back; two pillows were under her knees; and a smaller pillow she used at her feet to keep them from flopping down was also in place. Obviously, my mother had been home for a while. When Mrs. Gruder heard the tone of my mother's voice as she spoke to me, she started for the kitchen. "I'll just finish up a few things out there," she said.

"Why don't you go home, Eleanor?" my mother said, but she wasn't looking at Mrs. Gruder at all. Her eyes had not left me. "Go ahead and call Otto."

". . . All right, then." Mrs. Gruder went to the phone and dialed. Her number had a lot of zeros; I thought she'd never finish. "Come and get me now; I'll wait on the porch," I heard her tell Otto. She hung up the phone, and I heard the rustling sounds of her gathering up her things. Then, "Good night," she called out doubtfully, and my mother called back good night, again without taking her eyes from me.

After we heard the click of the front door, my mother said, "Come here, Diana."

I hesitated. "What. I'm here."

"I said, come here."

I stepped a bit closer to her bedside. She was still sitting up high; Mrs. Gruder had not yet lowered her to the forty-five-degree angle at which she slept. *"Here!"* she said angrily, and I moved to sit beside her.

She looked closely into my face for a long while, saying nothing. Then, "Light me a cigarette," she said, and I did, then held it up for her to puff on. All the while she smoked, she said nothing. Finally, I couldn't stand it any longer. *"What?!"* I said.

She drew in a last puff, exhaled over my head. "Finished."

I ground out the butt in the ashtray for what was perhaps too long a time, then turned back to her. "Do you want me to lower you down now? Do you want to sleep?"

"No." She worked at dislodging a piece of tobacco from her tongue. I picked it off and flicked it away.

"All gone," I said cheerfully.

"Where were you? And what did you drink?"

"What do you mean?"

"Diana."

I looked down. "I was at Suralee's. And she . . . just . . . made some drinks. Just for fun."

"What drinks?"

"Coke with a little rum, just a little." I looked up at her. "But did you have fun? On your date?"

My mother readjusted her head on her pillow. "No. I did not have fun. I was ridiculed and stared at. And then I was thrown out."

"Why?" I felt dangerously close to tears, but oddly, my sorrow was for me.

"It seems the proprietor had no idea about the extent of my disability. At first he didn't say much, just looked at me, you know that look?"

I made a pulled-in kind of face and my mother nodded. "Exactly," she said, with grim pleasure.

"And then sometimes they do like this," I said, and made a frankly horrified face, which made my mother smile. Maybe we were done with my sins and could move on to her humiliations.

"I'll tell you what happened next, Diana. Though I had my back to the rest of the room, as Brooks had promised, it seemed I was upsetting the other diners. They didn't like the noise of my respirator. They didn't like it that I had to be fed. One man came up to me on his way out. He said, 'What can you have been thinking, to come out to a public restaurant this way?' "

"What did you say?" I asked.

"At first, nothing," my mother said. "My mouth was full. I kept chewing and I just looked at him. *'Well?'* he said, and then he said it again, louder, so I spit my food out at him. And then I said, 'Sorry, my mouth was full. Now we can have a conversation.' "

I saw the scene, some scowling man standing before my mother while his indignant wife waited by the door, holding tightly on to her purse, her jaw dropping after my mother spit food at her husband.

"What did Brooks and Holt do?" I asked, giggling in a kind of loose way that let me know I was still not quite myself. I cleared my throat, overcorrected my posture.

"They escorted me out," my mother said. "Because right after that I was told to leave. And never to come back. But I will go back."

"Why?" I said. "Why would you ever want to go back there?"

Her respirator was on inspiration, but I could see the answer burning in her eyes. Then she said, "You know, it's so funny. What keeps any of those people in that dining room from being like me is just a virus, a thing in my body over which I had no control. Why did I get it and not them? Fate. Circumstance. Luck. But I have a place on the earth, just as they do. I have rights.

"When I was in the lung, I had people tell me every day that I had to get used to the fact that I could never have a normal life. Every day, they told me that I would have to come to terms with all I could no longer do." She shook her head, remembering. "But I decided to concentrate on what I *could* do. When the shrink talked about how the disease would affect my personality, I talked about how my personality would affect the disease. I didn't understand why nobody . . . I kept thinking, 'I am me! I am still *me*!' " Her voice began to shake, and she closed her eyes, then opened them. "Wipe my tears away and give me a chocolate," she said.

I put a tissue to her eyes and then lifted the box up so she could see in. "Which one?" I asked.

She surveyed the candies carefully.

"The chocolate-covered cherry?" I asked.

"The Messenger Boy," she said, and I gave it to her with regret. I put the box back down, hoping she would say, around her mouthful of chocolate, "You take one, too." But she did not. She chewed slowly, swallowed, and then, in a more deliberate tone, she began speaking again.

"I promised myself that I would raise you, though everyone advised me against it. I promised myself I would pay attention to the world and keep on learning, maybe go back to school someday, though I knew how hard it would be. I thought I might even get married again. Everyone, *everyone,* said I shouldn't get my hopes up for that kind of relationship. I've given up on that, but I learned tonight that I can at least go out. I can leave the house. It's scary, but I can do it. And maybe someday I will go back to school. I know I'll be looked at. I know it'll bother people to see me. I know most people would say I should stay home, where it's easier for me and my caretakers. But what most people think isn't always the right thing."

I sat still, hardly breathing. I had never heard my mother talk so much about this all at once. Everywhere around me, it seemed, people were saying odd, charged things.

"All your life, Diana, you're going to run into situations where you have to decide whether or not to take a stand. Sometimes it just isn't worth it. But other times it is. Not only is it worth it, it's vital. It makes you the person that you are. You have to honor what you know is true, or bit by bit, you die inside." She smiled. "So. Now let's talk about *your* evening."

Ah. "That's pretty much all," I said. "What I told you. It was just for fun, the rum. It was just a little. I didn't even like it, really. It made me feel sick. I won't do it again, I didn't even like it. So . . ." I leaned over to look at her clock and had to stop myself from falling on my face. "I think I'll go to bed."

"Oh, I think not," my mother said.

"Why not? I'm tired."

"Are you."

"Yes."

"Well, I'm not quite through talking to you. Let's talk some more. Who else was at Suralee's?"

How did she *know* these things? I considered lying, but she'd been all right about the rum. Maybe she just wanted to continue our mother-daughter talk—she was very talky tonight.

"Oh yeah, she had these two guys over."

"And where was Noreen?"

I wanted to say, *Well, you're so smart about these things, why don't you tell me?* Instead I said, "She wasn't there the *whole* time."

"Oh?"

"No, she had a date, so she wasn't there. The whole time."

"Uh-huh. And who are these boys?"

I know this one. "Just friends of Suralee's. She's known them a long time. They're brothers. They play baseball."

My mother waited.

"They're real nice."

"So the nice boys and you and Suralee had some drinks."

I stared into space, as if trying to remember.

"Diana."

"Yes!"

"Anything else happen?"

I stared at my hands. *The little prickly hairs of his blond crew cut, the way he smelled so good. How nice it was to be hugged. But the way he forced my mouth open when he kissed me and slung his tongue around, the way he stopped talking to me. The rocking motion of his hips against mine when we lay on the floor, so hard I thought he'd leave bruises.* "What do you mean?" I said.

"I mean, did anything else happen."

"Well, we talked. And . . . that's about it."

She said nothing, and I burst into tears.

"What happened?" she said, and in a rush, I told her. We kissed, he touched me, I threw up, Suralee got mad, I came home. That's all. The end.

My mother nodded. Then she said, "Well. You're growing up quickly, aren't you?"

I shrugged.

"It's wonderful to grow up—all these exciting adventures, all these new privileges."

I said nothing.

"Of course, with any privilege comes responsibility, wouldn't you say that's true?"

"I'm *really* tired. Can I just go to bed now? Can we just talk about this tomorrow?"

It was as though she hadn't heard me at all. "Now, in this case, we're talking about sex. Huh. I would have thought you were a bit young for that. But you've decided otherwise. Now, you told me this young man touched you. Did you like it?"

I was deeply embarrassed. "No."

"Is that all he did, was touch you?"

"Yes!"

"All right. Well, here's what I can tell you, Diana. You say you didn't like it. And maybe that's true."

"It is true!"

"But if you didn't like it this time, it doesn't mean you won't like it next time."

"What next time." My foot started wiggling, and I stopped it. I was now past giddiness and into a kind of ragged irritation. I really was tired; I so much wanted to go to bed. I was still dizzy, and I could feel some nausea returning.

"Oh, there will be a next time," she said. "And a time after that. And what you're going to have to know is how to handle yourself when those situations arise. Now, this time maybe you just felt awkward."

Not true. I had mostly liked it. I had felt on fire. At first, I had wanted him to never stop.

"But at some point," my mother said, "it's not going to feel awkward. And then you're really going to need some willpower. Do you think you have willpower?"

"I guess so."

"I don't think that answer is quite good enough, Diana. Because if you get in situations like that again and you don't have willpower, you'll go too far. And you'll end up in trouble. Believe me."

I looked at her, outraged. "I'm not going to get pregnant! I would never do that."

"Never say never," my mother said in a singsong way. I wondered, suddenly, if my mother had been pregnant when she got married. But I didn't want to ask, for all it would say about me.

"You've apparently decided that you can handle the pleasure of sex," my mother said. "I want to make sure you can handle the responsibility. So here's what I want you to do. I know you're really tired. I know you want to go to bed. What I want you to do is stay up for a few hours."

"What? *Why?*"

"Because you need to understand that sometimes your body is going to be asking you so hard for something and you're going to have to know how to not give in to it. This will give you an idea."

"Okay," I said. "I'll stay up for a few hours."

"And I'll stay up with you. You just stay there." She nodded. "You stay right there. But first get me a fresh drink of water. You might want one yourself. This is going to take awhile, and it's going to be hard."

And it was. Many times I went to the kitchen to splash cold water on my face so that I could wake up a little. A few times I told her I *got* it, I understood, could I just go to bed now. Each time she said no. Once, I took aspirin for the aches in my body. Nothing felt comfortable—not the floor, not the chair beside her bed.

We talked sometimes. The lights were out; I could see only the dim outline of my mother, and this, combined with the spaciness of extreme fatigue, made for a kind of freedom of inquiry. Once I asked her why, when she was in the iron lung, everyone was so pessimistic about what her life would be when she was discharged.

"They didn't want me to be disappointed," she said. "They were trying to be realistic. There was one crazy nurse there who made us all feel better, though. She looked at people who had polio as a privileged group, like a secret society. She said we had superior nervous systems, much more organized than most and therefore more susceptible to disease. She said such highly developed systems indicated great abilities or talents." She laughed. "Not that we could do anything with it. But for many, it was nice to believe."

"Did you believe it?" I asked.

She hesitated, then said, "Yes. Sometimes I did."

At another point, I asked her, "What's the hardest thing?"

"About what?" she asked.

"About . . . being you. The way you are now, I mean."

A long pause, and then she said, "When I went out tonight, we passed a rosebush, and there were petals on the ground beneath it. I wanted them. I used to sprinkle them places—in my bathwater, into little bowls around the house. I was thinking of how I'd like to have a bowl full of rose petals beside me at night, but I couldn't ask Brooks to stop and get some for me."

"Why? Was it too hard to talk?" She had a lot of difficulty talking when she was breathing on her own.

"No. Because it would have been too much to ask. You get a sense about what you can and cannot ask for. Brooks was already doing so much. He was nervous. He was gripping the wheel, and he had this little band of perspiration above his lip. He was just staring so hard at the road! I think Peacie scared the hell out of him.

"But anyway, it's . . . You know, if someone turns the television on for you, you can't ask them to flip through the channels during the commercials. If someone has just rearranged your limbs for you, you have to wait awhile before you ask them to do it again. That's what's hard. Those little aggravations. Peacie dusts and the lampshade is askew, but I can't be after her to straighten it."

"I don't see why you couldn't ask for *that.*"

"Oh, Diana. If you ask for everything you want, you'd be asking for things all day. Think, sometime, about the million little freewill things you do. And then think about having to ask someone to do every one of them for you. You'll see what I mean."

I sat still, imagining variations in my day brought about by my own whimsy. Sleeping late. Spreading a thick layer of peanut butter on my sandwich, because I was in the mood for more than usual. Stopping at the window at the bottom of the steps to watch the robin that landed on our lawn. Removing a barrette that was beginning to hurt my head. Going off somewhere to be alone.

"It's awful, isn't it," I said, quietly.

"It's what it is," my mother said. "And believe it or not, it has its positive side. It teaches you to be content with less. Otherwise, you'd go crazy."

I shuddered—a spasm of aggravation on her behalf. "What do you think you got it from? Do you really think it was from a water glass?"

"I do. I'll never know, of course." She looked at her bedside clock. One A.M. "All right; you can go to bed now."

"I don't want to yet."

She smiled. "Go to bed."

"I will, but . . . can we just talk some more?" There was something about this middle-of-the-night talking, an openness in and access to my mother I'd not enjoyed before.

"I just want to ask you something," I said. "Did you ever think . . . Did you ever wonder if you *caused* it, somehow?"

As soon as I spoke the words, I regretted them. But it was something I'd always wondered about.

"There was a six-year-old boy in a lung," she said. "I used to hear him talking to his mother. He used to say he was sorry, over and over, for playing with a dog he'd been told not to pet. It didn't matter how many times his mother told him he didn't catch polio that way; he believed he had."

"What about you?"

"I knew it was a virus. I knew it was. But sometimes I'd think . . . I'd wonder if it was punishment for being so wild."

"What do you mean?" I asked. "Being wild?"

"Oh, it was just crazy thinking. I did that sometimes, I guess everybody did. I wanted to have something to blame it on. But it was just a virus that attacked the motor-nerve cells of my spinal column. There was no reason. It was a long time ago. I need another drink of water, Diana."

I went into the kitchen and refilled her glass, and it came to me that the temperature of the water was up to me, and she would say nothing about it being too warm or too cold—she never had. I looked at my reflection in the window above the sink. Her daughter. I stared while the water ran over the top of the glass, and then I turned off the tap and brought the glass out to her, stuck the straw in, and let her drink. I wondered how long she'd been thirsty before she asked for anything.

We sat in silence for a long while after that. At one point I asked if she was asleep, and she said no. I heard her bedside clock ticking, the night wind blowing, the creaks of the house, the whirring of the fan, the usual sounds of her respirator, my own breathing. We shared the silence in a way that felt like talking.

Around three, she called my name, checking to see if I was still awake. "Why don't you go to sleep now?" she said. "I think you got the point."

"What was your very favorite thing to do when you were my age?" I asked.

She didn't answer for a while, weighing whether or not to let me stay up, I knew. Then she said, "I'll bet you'll be surprised at what my favorite thing to do was."

"Why? What was it?"

"I liked to make little tiny cities," she said. "Outside, in the dirt. I made roads, I built houses out of cardboard, I used wooden blocks for cars. I made telephone poles from branches and used my mama's black sewing thread for wires. I made holes in the ground and filled them with water for little lakes—my daddy would get so mad at me for digging holes."

"Were you afraid of him?" I asked.

"No," she said. "He wasn't a mean man, just *righteous,* you know? Church-righteous—that man never did sit any way but straight up in his chair. And my mama was a lot like him. I didn't feel . . . I guess I just never felt like I belonged to either of my parents. I mean, I *didn't* biologically, of course. But I didn't in any other way, either. It was just a bad fit."

"We're a good fit," I said, and she said yes we were.

A little after three, I felt an odd rush of energy. "I'm not tired anymore," I said.

"Yes you are," my mother said wearily.

"I'm not! I broke through it! I'm fine! Let me just finish the whole night, please? I can do it. I want to."

"All right," she said. "But you are tired, believe me." And then she told me about how when she worked nights as a nurse, the first night was awful. That there was always a point at which you thought you'd come out of the fatigue, but then it would come back, worse.

About this she was right, too. Just before six, I ached all over—even my kneecaps hurt. I felt nauseated again, too. I felt like I wanted to cry, but I didn't. I saw the sky lighten, and the birds begin to fly from branch to branch in the backyard. I had always thought of dawn as bursting forth, delivering a new day with Disneyesque optimism. I felt none of that now. Now I sat on a wooden chair by my mother's bedside, rubbing one arm and seeing the world as in resentful orbit, creaking and groaning as it forced into existence one more day. Here came the sun, starkly and uncaringly revealing our house, so small and different from the people's whose lives and fortunes were far better than our own. But I had done it; I had lasted the night.

When we heard Peacie coming through the door, my mother said, "All right. Now you really must go to bed." Her voice was croaky now, and she had deep circles under her eyes. She looked about as bad as I felt.

I started for the stairs, and Peacie narrowed her eyes at me. "What you up to?" she asked. I walked past her. "Vixen," she said, and then I heard her say to my mother, "Good God almighty, what happened to you?"

A little before noon, Peacie shook me awake. "Don't," I said. "I'm sick."

"You ain't sick. You hungover. Now wake up, I got to talk to you."

I squeezed my eyes shut and pulled the sheet up over my head. Peacie yanked it off and then grabbed me by the shoulders to sit me up. Reflexively, I reached out and slapped her. For a moment, we both sat still, staring wide-eyed at each other. I feared for myself. Surely she was going to slap me back, or worse.

But she only said, "Get dressed. Your mother is sick, she got to go the hospital. Riley ain't there, so I called over the hardware store. Brooks out to lunch, so Dell on the way over. You got to pack her things and help me get her in the car." She walked out of my room and quickly back downstairs. I lay still, listening to her talking to my mother, and heard my mother's weak voice, talking back. Then my mother began coughing. And coughing. I knew Peacie would be turning up the positive pressure on the respirator, forcing more air into my mother's lungs. If she didn't stop coughing, Peacie would have to fling herself across my mother's midsection to try to help bring up secretions.

My fault.

Outside, it rained. *Perfect.* I struck my chest with my fist, hit myself again. Then I got up, got dressed, and headed downstairs.

My mother was lying in bed, her eyes closed. Everything about her looked fragile and illuminated, like Mary in a holy card. "Mom?" I whispered.

She opened her eyes. "I'm fine."

She was not. I recognized the signs of respiratory distress: the labored exhalations, the sunken eyes, the off color.

"I'll pack some things for you," I told her. "Dell's going to take us to the hospital."

"Is he?" she asked, and closed her eyes again.

I packed quickly. Into the blue suitcase she kept under her bed I put her photo of me, her favorite lap quilt, and the bed socks she liked to use whenever she had to go into the hospital. Her medications and the complicated list of instructions for taking them. Her toothbrush and makeup. When I picked up her hairbrush, I began to cry. Peacie came into the room and spoke quietly. "You can shut them waterworks off right now. This ain't no way 'bout you. She got enough to worry about."

"It's all right, Peacie," my mother said, but her eyes stayed closed and she spoke as if she were in a dream. I hoped she was. I knew how much she hated going to hospitals. I wished she could stay asleep until she came home again. Somewhere around the edge of my brain a thought flitted in and out: She might not come home. This was how people with polio often died, a respiratory infection that couldn't be controlled. And this was the sickest I'd ever seen her.

Peacie had gone back into the kitchen to gather up her own things. I went to sit at the table. "Peacie?"

"What." She wouldn't look at me. I saw her anger in the flaring of her nostrils, in the deliberateness of her actions. I wanted to lie on the floor and prostrate myself, to beg for her forgiveness and, by extension of course, my mother's. Outside, thunder cracked as though someone were weighing in on the idea. Huge drops of water pelted the window.

I wanted to suggest that we put the shower curtain over my mother when we took her out, but instead I heard myself saying, "Is this because she stayed up all night? Is it my fault?"

Peacie turned to the sink to wash her hands, then to look at me, drying her hands slowly on her apron. She was chewing something—her anise seeds, I thought. She crossed her arms and raised an eyebrow, studying me. I sat still, my hands folded in my lap, an awful weight expanding inside me. Finally, she stopped chewing and spoke. "Well. Ain't that something, that overnight you done become God almighty. Ain't that something! Since you so powerful, maybe you can make it stop raining, it's gon' be hard enough, move her around. Now stop your useless fancyin' and come help me get her bundled up good—last thing she need is to get wet."

"Should we cover her with the shower curtain?" I asked.

"That's a good idea," Peacie said, and a breath I hadn't realized I'd been holding released itself. "Sometime your brain in good working order, give us both a shock. Go and get the curtain. And then go look out for Dell. When you see him, give a holler."

"Okay," I said, unhappy with the inadequacy of the simple phrase when my desire for service, for retribution, was so fierce. "I'll do it now!" I added.

"I don't believe I was talking 'bout you doing it next Friday," Peacie said.

I headed for the bathroom and heard Peacie saying, "Paige? *Paige?*"

I stopped dead in my tracks until I heard my mother respond. "Are we there?" she asked.

"Lord, Lord," Peacie muttered. "When that Dell *get* here?"

When I brought in the shower curtain and handed it to Peacie, my mother seemed more alert. "Get me a drink of orange juice, Diana," she said.

"I'll get it," Peacie said. "I want Diana watch for Dell. I want him get the car ready, we gon' take you right out. You gon' be just fine."

"Peacie," my mother said. "Take care of Diana."

"What you worrying yourself about? Don't worry 'bout a thing. You know I'm gon' take care Diana."

"Don't leave her alone," my mother said. There was a reaching quality to her voice, the equivalent of a hand on an arm.

"I ain't goin' to! I am well aware of recent developments that should not have been undertook by certain among us." Peacie looked over at me, her eyes like glittery black beads.

I stepped out onto the front porch, where rain drummed so powerfully I feared for the roof. Drops hit the asphalt hard enough to bounce up before they fell down again. Our yard was a gigantic mud puddle. Down the street I saw a van belonging to the hardware store coming quickly toward us, its windshield wipers thunking out a frantic rhythm. I knew that van—Brooks had used it to deliver our icebox to us. It had a ramp. We could roll her right up into the back and not have to transfer her from her wheelchair into a car seat.

"Dell's here!" I yelled. "He's got the van!"

"Tell him come in and help me lift her into the wheelchair," Peacie said. "I can't do it alone today."

"I'll help," I said, waving at Dell and holding up my finger, telling him to wait one minute.

"Not this time you can't," Peacie said.

I hesitated, then motioned to Dell to come inside. He rushed past without even looking at me. It made me sick how that hurt my feelings, how even now I could not keep myself from the center of things.

The phone rang and Peacie yelled, "Answer it. Might be the doctor."

It was not. It was Suralee, and I told her I'd call her back.

"When?" she asked, and I said I didn't know, I had to go.

"Oh, come on, get over it," she said.

I hung up.

Many hours later, at Peacie's house, I lay on her sofa, weeping. I cried about how my mother had looked when the nurses transferred her to the bed in the emergency room, her eyelids half closed, her brows knitted with the effort of breathing. I cried about how kind Dell had been, how when he'd come into the house, he'd leaned down and put his hand to the side of my mother's face, looked into her eyes, and said, *Hey there,* so gently. He'd lifted her into the wheelchair by himself. Then, after he got her into the van, he'd jumped into the driver's seat to take us quickly to the hospital, where he waited with us for hours.

I cried over the fact that LaRue wasn't going to be home until tomorrow, and here I was with Peacie with no buffer at all. I cried over how sick I felt; my head throbbed, my stomach ached. But mostly, I cried about my selfishness and pride, which, to my mind, had brought this on. I hated the front of me and I hated the back of me.

Finally, I had no tears left. I sat up and looked around the tiny living room. In addition to the sofa, there were two armchairs, dressed with doilies. A small footstool sat in front of one of the chairs; an end table was placed between them. On the table was a worn Bible, an empty ashtray, and a small lit lamp with a ruffled shade. There was a rag rug and a wooden crate holding magazines. A framed photograph hung on the wall, some colored woman in a dress with a high collar. She wore rimless glasses, and she was not smiling. Rather, she wore a fierce expression much like the one Peacie often had, only worse. I stared at her face and the hairs on the back of my neck rose.

I went into the kitchen, smaller than our own, but with a nicer-looking refrigerator. Peacie sat at a square metal table, playing solitaire. I sat opposite her and surveyed the cards. "Black eight on the red nine," I said, pointing.

"I know that," she said, and moved the card. Then she sat still, considering. I saw another move but kept my mouth shut. In a moment she saw it, too.

"Bet you's bustin' tell me 'bout that one, too."

"Didn't see it," I said.

"Lie like a rug." She leaned back in her chair and regarded me. "You 'bout done with your own private wailing wall?"

I nodded.

"Then get back in there and wring out that sofa 'fore it float away."

I smiled at Peacie, grateful for her attempt at humor. Behind her, at the window, were some yellow curtains with little white polka dots, tied back with matching bows. I recognized them as having been in a recent donation bag. "Are those from us?" I asked.

Peacie looked behind her. "What? The curtains?"

I nodded.

"Y'all gave them to me. Y'all didn't want them."

"They're pretty."

"You ain't taking them back. Ain't from you, anyway. They from your mother."

"I didn't say I wanted them. I said they were pretty."

She stood and pushed her chair in, leaned close to my face. "I see you coming and going, Diana Dunn."

She was right. I did want the curtains back. When we'd given them to her, they were wrinkled and dirty, raglike. Now they seemed cheerful and sweet.

"You hungry?" Peacie asked.

"No." We'd eaten from the vending machine at the hospital, chips and candy bars and packages of crackers and cheese.

"I believe I'll check in on your mother, then."

She was overly casual saying this; it made me worried. Peacie went to the wall phone and dialed a number, then straightened as she spoke into the mouthpiece. "Yes, I'm calling to inquire about a patient y'all have there, Miss Paige Dunn, room 507 . . . Yes, ma'am." She waited, her fingers drumming on the counter, then said, "Yes? . . . Yes, ma'am, I am a relative, I'm her sister, Betty Dunn, from New Orleans, calling long distance, so—yes . . . Oh, really, when was that? . . . I see. . . . All right, then, I'll try later." Peacie hung up the phone, went to the already clean sink, and started wiping at it.

"What," I said.

"What, 'what'?" She wouldn't turn around.

"What did they say at the hospital?"

"They say call back later, which I will do."

"Why didn't you talk to my mother?"

She didn't answer.

"Peacie?"

She turned around. "Now don't be carrying on. She went to the ICU. Cain't talk to her now."

I swallowed, then stood up. "Let's go. I want to go there."

Peacie came over to the table and pushed me gently back down into the chair. "Now look here at me. You know same as me we cain't go in there. She gon' be fine. She in the best place she can be at. You know she do this sometime, get all sick and then she come home fine as pie, ain't nothing to it."

"If she's in the ICU, she's *really* sick!"

"Well, where you want her to be if she that sick! The ICU! ICU mean . . . Instant Cure Underway, that is exact and precise what it mean."

"It means Intensive Care Unit. And half those people never come out." We stared at each other and then, miserable, I said, "When are you calling back?"

Peacie thought for a moment, then said, "Can you be a doctor?"

"What do you mean?"

"I mean can you call and act out you a doctor? Just like the play. Then they tell us how she is exactly."

I was seized by fear, but in a calm voice I answered, "Yes. I can do that."

Peacie handed me the phone and began dialing the number again.

"But what do I say?" I whispered.

She shrugged. "You the doctor."

When the hospital operator answered, I lowered my voice and identified myself as Dr. Halloway, then asked for the ICU. When a woman there answered "ICU" in a quick and nearly breathless way, I said, "Yes. Yes! I'm Dr. Halloway, calling to inquire about my patient, Paige Dunn."

"Yes, Doctor?"

"Uh . . ." I leaned against the counter, frozen and wild-eyed.

"How she doing," Peacie whispered. "How she *do*ing?"

"How . . . is she doing?"

"She's stable, Doctor. Spiked a temp up to a hundred and four, but we've got her on a cooling blanket and it's down to a hundred one.

She's a little tachycardic, but her pressure's back up and the other vital signs are okay. Urine output's fine. Sputum results aren't back yet, of course."

"Of course, of course," I said. "And when do you expect she'll come home?"

There was a pause, and then the woman said, "Well . . . that will be up to you, of course. . . . Did you say you were Dr. Halloway?" I could hear her rifling through some pages. "Are you on staff here?"

I hung up. "Her temperature was high, but it came down," I told Peacie. "She's on a cooling blanket."

Peacie nodded. "All right. Good. We call back later, *Doctor.*"

"I don't want to be the doctor anymore," I said. "You do it next time."

"You should feel better, Diana. That's the right direction she going in! That's good news we got." She laughed. "*Dr. Halloway!* Hey, Doctor, I got a pain in my Archilly heel, can you fix it?"

There was a loud knock on the door, and Peacie looked up at the kitchen clock. Nine-thirty. "Stay here," she told me, and went out into the living room.

"Good evening," I heard her say. "How you doing this evening?"

Good evening? I went to the threshold of the kitchen to see who had come. It was Sheriff Turner at the door. His hat was far back on his head, and he stood with his legs far apart, his hands on his hips. He was a handsome man, but he always made me feel squirmy inside.

"LaRue around?" he asked Peacie.

"No sir, he ain't."

"Where's he at?"

"He visiting his people."

"Where?"

"I . . . don't quite remember. I had some excitement with Miss Dunn today, had to take her to the hospital."

"Paige is in the hospital again?"

"Yassuh. Sho' is."

Yassuh?

"Well, I'm sorry to hear that. But I need to know where LaRue is, Peacie. I'm going to stand here and smoke a cigarette, and maybe it'll come to you. If not . . ." He shrugged. "Guess I'll smoke another one."

I watched Peacie's back for some give-away sign. Nothing. She stood silent, then finally bowed her head and said, "Meridian. Is he all right?"

"Well, that's something I want to pass on to you, Miss Peacie. If he's over there helping those college boys, he ain't going to be all right, I can guarantee you that. If he's helping those college boys, he might not come home at all."

"He coming home tomorrow!" Peacie said. It shot out of her so fast, I wasn't sure she meant to say it.

The sheriff leaned against the door frame. "Well, now. That's what I was waiting for. That's the kind of cooperation I want to see. When LaRue gets home, I want you to have him come and see me. I want to have a few words with him."

"I'll tell him."

"You won't forget now, will you, Peacie? You'll tell him to come on over and see me right away."

"Yassuh." Her head bobbing, her back bowed. "I sho' 'nuff will."

The sheriff turned to go, then turned back. "Now, you know I like LaRue, don't you? I got no ax with him."

"Yassuh."

"It's just I don't want to see him in no trouble with anybody else."

"No suh. Me neither!"

He chuckled. "So you just—" He spied me and stopped talking, leaned around Peacie for a better look. My heart sank. I hadn't done what Peacie had asked. "Who's that?" he asked her.

Peacie spun around, murder in her eyes. But when she turned back to the sheriff, her voice was sweet and low. "Why, you know, that's just

Diana, Miss Paige Dunn's daughter. I'm keeping her here with me while her mother in the hospital. Didn't want to leave her alone over her house."

"There wasn't anyone else who could take her?"

"Her mama want me to have her, ax me in the particular."

Sheriff Turner smiled and nodded at me, and I smiled back.

"This ain't no place for a white child," he told Peacie quietly.

"Yassuh," she said.

"Ain't no place for a white child! 'Specially at night."

"I be taking her home tomorrow."

"Why didn't you just stay at her house with her?"

"I needed to come home and feed my chickens and pack some things."

So Peacie believed my mother would be hospitalized for some time.

The sheriff stood still for a moment, thinking, then again stretched his head around Peacie to call out, "Diana! Come on over here!"

I walked slowly to the door, held up my hand in a weak wave. "Hi," I said.

"I understand your mother's in the hospital," he said.

"Yes, sir." The top of his undershirt was a yellowish color that Peacie would never have tolerated.

"Well, I'm real sorry about that. But I don't think it's a good idea for you to be here, do you? I'll tell you what, how about if you come home with me, I got a daughter 'bout your age."

"No, thanks. I want to stay here."

"Well . . . How old are you?"

"Going on fourteen."

"Eighth grade?"

"Yes, sir."

"So you know my daughter! K.C. Turner!"

Of course I knew her. Everyone knew her. "No," I said.

"You don't know K.C. Turner?"

I shook my head. "Nope."

"Well, I'm surprised!" He looked at Peacie as though she, too, should share his incredulity. She pretended to, shaking her head and smiling. "She's a real popular girl!" he said.

"It's a big school," I said.

He smiled. "Oh, it is, huh?"

"Sometimes it is," I said. "Right now it is."

"Well, I'm not going to . . ." The sheriff turned to Peacie. "I want that girl back in her own neighborhood tomorrow morning. Otherwise, we'll both be in trouble. You know that, don't you."

"Yassuh."

"I'll send someone take y'all back over there first thing."

"No suh, thank you very kindly, LaRue carry us."

"I don't want to see her back here," he said, and walked to his car, then slowly drove away.

Peacie closed the door, and I said, "I'm sorry. I was just trying to see."

"Don't make no never mind," she said, and I saw that she was too distracted to pay attention to my misdeed.

"Is LaRue in trouble?" I asked.

"He be home tomorrow," she said, by way of an answer. "And he ain't going back." She said that, but I wondered.

We walked together into the living room. Peacie sat in one of the chairs, staring into space, her fingers pulling at her bottom lip. I sat on the sofa, watching her.

Finally, "How come you talked that way to the sheriff?" I asked.

She said nothing.

"Peacie?"

"Hush now!"

I sat quietly for a long while, thinking about how I was somewhere I wasn't supposed to be. Was it dangerous? Was it just wrong? It was a

Negro house, but it was also just a house, much like my own. What trouble could come from my being here? Who could get hurt—me or Peacie? It was so odd, how it was one thing for Peacie and me to be together in my house, another thing entirely for us to be here.

I wondered about LaRue, wondered if he was in danger or would disappear as those three boys had. Then I began wondering about my mother. How long would she be gone? Something dark began to flower inside me; I had to talk against the feeling.

"Peacie?" I said. "Is this the worst you've ever seen my mom?"

She looked over at me. Then, regretfully, she said, "Yes."

I swallowed dryly. "So . . . is she going to die?"

Peacie waved her hand dismissively. "No! No, she ain't gon' die, foolish! She young and she a fighter. You know that same as me! She be better soon. She can't die, she got to finish raising you up. She knows ain't *nobody* else stand up for that!"

A long pause, and then in a small voice, I said, "You would . . . wouldn't you?"

Peacie hesitated, then came over to embrace me, the only time she ever had. And what I felt in that embrace was the knowledge that she would never be able to raise me, not by herself. I realized for the first time how alone I would be if my mother did die. How I would turn around and turn around and no one would be there. And all along, I'd thought it was my mother who so much needed me.

Peacie let go of me and looked into my face. "You go to sleep now," she said. "I'll get you some sheets for this here swimming pool you done made yourself. You be all right then?"

"Yassuh!"

She stared at me, her hand on her hip. "You think that's Negro talk? That's white-folk talk. You think about it. We do that for y'all."

"Sho' 'nuff?"

She smiled. "You your mother's daughter."

I felt singed by pride. When Peacie went off for the sheets, I sat on the sofa and drew my knees up to my chest, pushed my face against my knees, closed my eyes, and rocked back and forth.

Peacie came back and laid the sheets and a pillow at my feet. "Make up a bed for yourself," she said.

"I will."

"You need help?"

"No, thanks."

She turned out the living room light and spoke in the darkness. "She be much better tomorrow."

"I know."

"Lie down now, and go to sleep."

"I will." But I sat up for a long time, watching for something I couldn't name.

I awakened to the beautiful sound of LaRue's voice. " 'Course I's scared," he said. "We all of us was! One time, they come after us when we trying to march, come after us with clubs. When that happen, we s'pose to crouch down, protect our business, and put our hands up over the back of our necks. And then here they come, yelling and cussing, hitting on us again and again even though we ain't doing nothing back, we ain't doing nothing at all 'cept just trying to protect ourselves. I be staring at the ground, this one little spot. I didn't get it too bad, but the guy next to me did. And he lost control his facilities. He felt some bad, but I said, 'That's all right, you just speaking for all of us.' "

There was the sound of a chair pushing back, then the rattle of dishes and water running. "I'm glad you ain't going back there," Peacie said.

"What you mean?"

The water stopped, and there was a long silence. Then Peacie said, "I mean you ain't going back there. And I'm glad. Trouble enough here, you ain't need to be looking for it elsewheres."

"Peacie," LaRue said, and she said quickly, "No."

"Peacie," he said again.

"No!"

"I come home to help you today," he said, "but tomorrow I be going back."

I sat up slowly on the sofa and unstuck my pajama top from my back, listening to hear how Peacie would respond.

"We gon' move," she said.

I stopped breathing.

"Up by my aunt in Ohio. This time I mean it, we gon' move up there."

LaRue spoke softly. "You know, when I was a boy, my mama told me evil spirits hung men from trees. She told me be careful, don't let the evil spirits get me. I believed her and I was careful. I kept my eyes ahead of me, and I invite the Lord inside me, help me mind my own self. After I growed up and realized wasn't no evil spirits doing the lynching and the Lord ain't living too close by, I still stayed careful. But I cain't do that no more. I cain't quit this, Peacie. I seen some things I ain't never forget, and I'm gon' back help Li'l Bit finish what he start."

"They killing people!" Peacie said. "Every day! Bodies washed up on the riverbank, folks killed sleeping in they own bed!"

"Lot of ways to die," LaRue said. "Some of 'em better than others. I been changed, Peacie, I come to see—"

"Stay here and see!"

"No. No, I cain't. I started something there, and I got to finish it there. I be dug in."

"LaRue, somebody find out what you doin' and you gon' lose your job!"

"Well. I did lose my job."

The phone rang and Peacie answered it. "Yassuh, he here," she said, and then I heard LaRue telling the sheriff he'd be taking me home and then he'd stop on by, he'd be there within the hour. But after he hung up, he told Peacie, "I ain't going."

Silence.

I stood and cleared my throat, announcing the fact that I was awake. Then I came out into the kitchen. "Hey, Diana," LaRue said, smiling. "How you doin', baby?" It was so good to see him sitting there cross-legged in his neatly pressed trousers, his short-sleeved white shirt, his bright yellow suspenders. His hat lay on the table before him, and I wished suddenly that I could have it.

"Get dressed," Peacie told me. "We gon' take you home." She leaned past LaRue to clear the table of the rest of the dishes and did not look at him. When he reached out and gently grabbed her, she pulled away in a manner not gentle at all.

When I got home, Suralee was sitting with Shooter on my front-porch steps. Peacie went straight into the house; I sat wordlessly beside Suralee. I did not look at her. For a long while, neither of us spoke. Then Suralee said, "Sorry about what happened at my house."

"It doesn't matter," I said.

"Is your mom better?"

Now I did look at her. "How'd you know?"

She shrugged. "Everybody does."

"She's still in the ICU." I felt tears starting in my eyes. Peacie had called Brenda, suggesting she might want to come. It couldn't be a good sign.

"Want to stay with me?" Suralee asked. She had traces of purple at the edges of her mouth. I guessed she'd been drinking grape Nehi, our favorite flavor.

"No, thanks. Peacie's going to be here with me."

Suralee rubbed the back of Shooter's neck. "Then can I stay with y'all?"

We laughed, but I knew she meant it.

Suralee leaned back on her elbows, surveyed the empty street before us, and sighed. My mother always said that if you were bored, it was your fault, but it seemed to me that sometimes boredom came from the outside in. This town could feel like someone putting a high pile of cinder blocks on your chest, then saying, "Okay, breathe."

Suralee sat up suddenly. "Oh! I almost forgot! Did you get something from the contest?"

"What do you mean?"

"That contest we entered, did you win anything?"

"No, did you?"

"Yeah. But only a box of crackers and one of cookies." She shrugged. "They came in the mail yesterday. I might could share them with you." This last she spoke quietly.

"That's okay."

I could feel her relief. "That's how I think of it, too. Whoever wins something should just feel happy, and all their friends be happy for them, too."

"Right." All Suralee's friends being me.

"Anyway, it wasn't that much."

"It's something, though. Congratulations."

"I was a little bit afraid to tell you. I didn't want you to feel bad."

"Don't worry, I don't." I'd known neither of us would win anything good. We never had. We never would. We were not that kind of people.

A horn sounded, and I saw Dell's car coming down the street. He slowed and pulled over to the curb. "How is she?" he called.

I walked over to him. "She's still real sick."

He nodded, his smile fading. "Call me when she comes home. I'd like to come and see her."

I said I would.

I walked back to the porch and sprawled out beside Suralee. "What do you want to do today?" I asked.

"He really likes your mom," she said.

I looked at her.

"He does!"

"But what do you want to do today?" Absent the necessity of taking care of my mother, the day seemed too big, too bright, too empty.

"You want to come over to my house?" Suralee asked. "We could start a new play."

"Let's go downtown," I said. I didn't want to return to the scene of the crime.

I went into the house to tell Peacie I was leaving. She was standing at the washing machine, and she did not turn around to tell me it was all right for me to go. Instead, she simply nodded. "You okay?" I asked. She nodded again, then waved me away.

Suralee and I went first to Debby's Dress Shop, where we wanted to try on the pillbox hats. "Y'all put those down," Mrs. Black said from behind the counter. "You have no intention of buying them, and I can't have them getting soiled."

"We were going to buy one," Suralee said. "For Diana's mom."

She looked doubtfully at us.

"I got the money right here," I said, patting my empty pocket. "But I believe I'll take my business elsewhere."

"You do that," Mrs. Black said, and smiled at a woman coming through the door.

We crossed the street to the drugstore, where Mrs. Beasley asked the inevitable question. "She's better," I said, not meeting her eyes.

"Bless your heart," Mrs. Beasley said, and I said, "Yes, ma'am."

Suralee and I looked at shampoos for a while, unscrewing the caps to smell the delectable scents of the more expensive brands. We used

White Rain and White Rain only; I found it uninspiring. Peacie occasionally used beer as a rinse for my mother's hair; it did seem to make it more lustrous. She was also a big believer in mayonnaise treatments, but my mother said mayonnaise was too expensive to waste that way.

From behind the counter came Mrs. Beasley's thin voice: "Y'all aren't taking the caps off the shampoos, are you?" she said. "Don't be doing that now. Nobody wants to buy shampoo been fooled with."

"We're not," we sang out together, and moved to the magazine stand. We sat back-to-back, thumbing through the usual picks, and I said to Suralee, "When I grow up, I am moving to a town where there is so much to do it makes you sick."

"I know. Memphis."

"No," I said. "Even more."

"Right. Someplace where"—Suralee leaned back against me, harder, and here came her English accent—"Oh, what to do this evening! So many choices, what a bloody bother! Harold, darling. Bring me some tea, I must cogitate."

Suralee's mother had given her some money, and we shared a patty melt and a Coke at the lunch counter, then went over to the hardware store. Though neither of us directly acknowledged it, we were looking for Dell.

I didn't see him when we came in, but Brooks was positioning a sign at the front of the store and he waved me over. "How is she?" he asked, and I told him she was still in the ICU. He nodded sadly. "What can I buy her, do you think?" he asked. "I'd like to buy her something, cheer her up." I said I didn't know.

"We were looking at pillbox hats for her," Suralee told him. "Every woman wants one of those."

"Is that right?"

"Mrs. Black wouldn't let us touch them, but I think they're real soft."

Brooks stared out the window at her store, then said, "Well, let's just go and have a look-see." He called over to one of the other men, saying he'd be back in a few.

Suralee and I followed Brooks across the street, Shooter walking behind us. I wished we could sic him on Mrs. Black. But I had noticed graying on the dog's muzzle when he lay on my porch that morning; Suralee said it had been there for a while, and that Shooter was starting to sleep a lot more than he used to. It seemed unfair that a dog so fierce and self-contained should suffer the indignity of growing old like any other dog. I would rather see Shooter die young; I thought he himself would prefer that.

It was strange seeing Brooks in the dress shop. It was a small and feminine place with pink walls and white trim; he didn't fit there. But Mrs. Black couldn't have been more polite. "Well, *hi,* Brooks," she said, like he was her long-lost relative, even though she surely saw him on the street every day. "What can I do for you?" She looked quickly at us and then away.

"I'm interested in one of them pill hats," Brooks said.

"Oh yes," she said, moving over to her display. "Aren't they just the most elegant thing? I'm 'bout running out, they're so popular. But I have three left, as you can see. What color were you thinking of?"

"I was thinking 'bout all the colors," Brooks said. "I was thinking I'd buy every hat you have."

"For heaven's sake, Brooks!" she said, giggling, pressing her manicured fingers into her breastbone.

"And also I was thinking you got no call to be treating these girls like you do."

She stopped smiling and crossed her arms. "Well, I don't know how much time they spend at *your* establishment messing with the merchandise with no intention of buying one single thing, but I—"

"They're welcome at my store when they ain't buying shit." He wiped at his nose and shifted his position, putting his hand to his hip like football players did. "Either one of them, Diana or . . . her friend."

"Suralee," I whispered quietly behind him.

"Shir*ley,*" he said.

"Did you want to buy something or not?" Mrs. Black asked.

"Believe I said I did," Brooks answered.

"You want every hat I've got."

"Every *pill* hat."

"It's pill*box.*"

"It's a stupid name either way," Brooks said. "It's just a hat. Now I'm going to pay you, and then suppose you wrap up those hats real nice and give them to these girls. I believe you could call them customers now, couldn't you? What with they being the ones sent me over here. I believe you could treat them with some respect."

"Cash or check?" Mrs. Black asked coolly, and Brooks pulled out his wallet, and from it a check. His wallet was greatly worn; it curved up in the corners. What I knew about Brooks was that he could afford three hats little more than we could. I wanted to thank him for his extravagance but couldn't find the words. I watched him write the check; he was left-handed, and he wrote with his hand above the moving pen. It was like a bear taking penmanship classes. I moved from behind my instinctive dislike of him to see a man in a thin blue shirt with a worn collar making an offering of love against fear. I had done it myself, determinedly made cards for my mother thinking that she would then have to stay alive to read them.

My mother stayed in the ICU for two days, then was moved to a general floor. Peacie and I took the bus to visit her, toting our Scrabble board. We set up a game, and when Peacie put GNU on the board, I said, "No. I challenge that." I reached for the paperback dictionary we'd brought along, its pages curled from use.

"Go right ahead and challenge it, it's a word!" Peacie said.

"Meaning what?" I asked.

Peacie straightened in her chair and spoke slowly and clearly. " 'Either of two African antelopes. Having a drooping mane. And beard. And a long, tufted tail.' " She said all the *A*'s with the long sound. Obviously the word had come up before. She leaned forward to add, "Also called a wild beast. Like you."

"Well, *wildebeest,*" my mother said gently.

I scowled and gave Peacie her points, and my mother laughed. She was in high spirits, so happy to be out of the confining and desperate atmosphere of the ICU, every day closer to coming home. Yesterday Brenda had taken time off work to spend the whole day with my mother. She had fed her homemade macaroni and cheese for breakfast, made the way my mother liked it, with extra cheese and little bits of bacon and tomato mixed in. They'd ordered out chow mein for lunch and pizza for dinner. Later that night, before she went home, Brenda lay in bed with my mother to watch television and drink the beers she had smuggled in in her purse and kept cold in my mother's ice pitcher, which she then hid in the bedside cabinet. "Where's your ice pitcher?" the candy striper had asked that afternoon when she came to refill it.

"I must have left it somewhere when I went for my walk," my mother had replied.

"Okay, I'll get you another one, don't worry," the candy striper had said, and my mother had said, "Okay, I won't."

Twice, the nurse caring for my mother in the evening had ordered Brenda out of my mother's bed; twice, Brenda had complied and then, after the nurse left, climbed right back in with her.

While my mother was ordinarily a deeply kind person, her mischievous tendencies came out in the hospital. Today, when the robust nurse taking care of her came to take her temperature, she put the thermometer in my mother's mouth and left the room, saying she'd be right back to collect it. My mother did one of her old tricks: used her tongue to turn the thermometer around backward. When the nurse came back in, she blushed and said, "Well, for heaven's sake, I'm sorry, I put it in backwards! Let's do this again." She put the thermometer in the right way, left the room again, and when she came back it was backward again. This time she stood holding the thermometer and glaring at my mother. "I don't have time for this, Miss Dunn," she said.

To which my mother responded, "That's okay, Miss Carson; I do." The nurse's wrath grew, and my mother said, "Now now; don't get nasty or I won't do it again."

On the day of discharge, Brooks helped us bring my mother home. She had lost weight, but in many respects she was more beautiful than ever. Her hair was shiny from her hospital shampoo ("Castile soap—they use it for enemas, but it's great for your hair," she told us). Her eyes were bright, the skin of her face beautifully colored and flawless. She always enjoyed a certain vitality when she came home from hospital visits; she had defied the odds once again, and she relished the victory.

After she was settled inside, sitting in her wheelchair in the living room, Brooks set his gift on her lap. I opened it for her, and she stared wide-eyed, smiling, and then had Brooks put all three pillbox hats on her, one stacked up on top of the other. She thanked him profusely, though I could tell she wondered why in the world he had made such a purchase. I did not enlighten her.

Then Peacie went off to do chores, and I started upstairs. Brooks was finally left alone with my mother, something I knew he'd been waiting for, and for once I didn't begrudge him the pleasure of her company. "How's Dell?" she asked.

I stood still at the landing to listen for Brooks's response. After a weighted pause, I heard him say, "He's fine." The tone of his voice made me believe he was hanging his head, and I felt sorry for him. But I resolved to go and see Dell later that afternoon to let him know my mother was back—I didn't think Brooks would be in any hurry to do so.

When I came downstairs, Brooks had gone, and Peacie and my mother were in the kitchen, talking in low voices. "If he don't get killed, I might shoot him myself," Peacie said.

"Does he call every day?" my mother asked.

"Sometime he do and sometime he don't," Peacie said. "Either way make me mad. I don't know why he got to march, he doing enough with the Freedom Schools."

"There are injunctions prohibiting demonstrations now," my mother said.

"That's right," Peacie said. "But they doing them anyway. And any Negro participate or even watch can get arrested. Now how I'm gon' get him out if he get arrested?"

"He won't get arrested," my mother said. "He's too smart for that. And too charming."

"He get arrested, he can rot in jail," Peacie said, "and I find me a new boyfriend don't go running off and get in trouble on purpose, act like a fool. I find me a young man, take me dancing."

My mother remained tactfully silent, and I made my presence known, coming into the room and asking what was for lunch.

Peacie looked over at me. "How those broken hands of yours coming along?" she asked.

The next afternoon, while my mother was napping, I sat at the kitchen table working on a scene for Suralee and my new play, a drama involving the murder of a dress-shop owner. We'd been benignly arguing over who got to play the killer. Peacie came up from the basement and asked me to go into town for detergent. "We still have some," I told her.

"We need more," Peacie said.

"There was almost half a box this morning; I saw it. There's got to be enough left for today." *Strangled by a scarf?* I was thinking. *Beaten about the head with a pocketbook?*

Peacie dragged a chair out from under the table and sat close to me. She snatched away the paper I was writing on and crinkled it up.

"Hey!" I reached out to take the paper back.

She threw it on the floor, then leaned forward and spoke quietly. "Diana Dunn, you made of stubbornness, you know that? That's all you are. You ain't got no guts inside, just stubbornness. 'Fore I die, maybe you cooperate on one single thing. 'Fore I die, I like to say, 'Diana, would you bring in the sheets on the line?' and you say, 'Yes, ma'am, I do it right now on account of I *owe* it to you.' " Tears sprung up suddenly in her eyes and began to roll down her face; she brushed them aside angrily. " 'I owe it to you, for all the things you do for me. Things I ain't even *know* about.' " She struck out at the air and began to cry harder, and I sat watching her, slump-shouldered and miserable. I would have felt better if she'd made contact, if she'd hit me.

"Someday I like you to know all I done give up, take care you and your mother. I could have left here long time ago, me and LaRue both, but I stay on account of y'all. And this what I get in return, some Jesus-size argument for ever' single thing I say. You 'bout wore me out, Diana."

"I'll go to the store," I said. "I'm sorry. I'll go."

"You think you—"

The phone rang and Peacie leapt up for it. LaRue hadn't called in three days; I hoped this was him now. But the call was for my mother. "Yes, this the right number, but she be napping right now," Peacie said. She pulled a man's-sized handkerchief from her apron pocket and pressed it against her nose, sniffing. She listened intently, then straightened and said, "Hold on." She put her hand over the mouthpiece and whispered, "Did your mother enter a contest?"

I nodded, then whispered back, "I entered for her. She doesn't know."

Peacie looked at me for a long moment. Then she said, "She done won second prize."

I stood, my heart pounding. Peacie pressed her hand to her mouth, and from behind it came a high-pitched squeal. She closed her eyes and took in a breath, smoothed down the front of her apron. Then, into the phone, she said, "Could you please wait just one minute? I'm gon' wake her up."

Peacie held the phone out to me and in an overly controlled voice said, "I'm gon' go tell her."

I held the phone pressed to my breast in a mix of impatience and fear. What if the call got disconnected? What if you lost the prize if you didn't accept it soon enough after they called? What if there was a giant ticking clock on a wall, moving closer to them calling the next person on the list? Then my insides sagged. This was a joke. I put the phone up to my ear to listen. I heard nothing. "Suralee?" I said.

"Yes, hello?" an unfamiliar voice said. "Is this Paige Dunn?" I said no, but she was coming, just one second, she'd be right there, could they hold on just one more second? Then, after Peacie pushed my mother up to the phone, I pressed the receiver to her ear.

"Hello?" she said. "Yes, this is Paige Dunn." Then she looked up at me while she said, "You . . . you're kidding. You're kidding, right?" She listened some more, the color rising in her face, gave out our address, listened some more, and then said good-bye. "We won twenty-five hundred dollars," she said. "We won *twenty-five hundred dollars*!"

"Lord have mercy!" Peacie shrieked, and I pounded on the kitchen table so hard I hurt my hand.

"They want to come and take my picture tomorrow," my mother said. "All I have to do is sign some papers and they'll give me the check." Something occurred to her. "Won't *they* be surprised!" she said.

I got up before Peacie arrived, and crept downstairs to my mother's bedroom. She was awake, and she smiled at me. "Come here," she said. "I'm so excited I hardly slept. You know what I'm going to buy you? I'm going to buy you a canopied bed. And a whole new wardrobe. And any game you want. And I'm going to buy myself a Royal electric typewriter. I'll press the keys with a pencil."

I climbed into her bed and lay beside her. She kissed the top of my head. Her breath was terrible—we'd had garlic bread with last night's dinner. "Peacie needs to brush your teeth really good this morning," I said.

She opened her mouth wide and blew down on me. "Yours isn't much better," she said.

I blew back into her face and we laughed.

"*And* we're going to hire a nighttime caretaker," she said.

"Can we get Lay's potato chips now?" I asked, and my mother said, "Nothing but."

"What are you going to wear for the picture?" I asked.

"I don't know, what do you think?"

"Something blue," I said.

"Okay. Maybe my blue blouse. And if they can take the picture from above the vent hose up, I could look normal. What are you going to wear?"

"Me? I don't know. They're not taking my picture."

"They might. They ought to. You're the one who really won."

"Yeah, but don't tell them," I said.

"Believe me!"

I reached over and picked up one of my mother's plaster shells. She had two, so that one could air out when she wore the other. I laid it over myself. "I think I'll wear this," I said. "I'll put flowers in the vent hole."

"Take that off," my mother said.

I smiled. "Not my style?"

"Take it off!" she said, with a ferocity that stunned me.

I laid the shell aside, then said, "I'm not going to get polio, you know."

"That's right," my mother said. "And you won't ever put that shell on again, either." She looked over at the bedside clock. "Wonder where Peacie is? She's never late. And especially today, she needs to be on time."

"I'll get you started," I said.

My mother hesitated, then said, "I need the bedpan."

"Okay."

"Put it under me and then go out of the room," she said, and I said I knew. "Give Peacie a call," my mother said. "Maybe she overslept."

I went into the kitchen and dialed Peacie's number. There was no answer. "She's on the way," I called.

I felt bad for Peacie. It would hurt her pride to arrive late. I'd pretend I didn't notice. I opened the cupboard to survey the breakfast cereals. Soon we'd be able to buy any kind we wanted. I felt a rush of excitement close to a convulsion, and then my mother called, "Diana? Done."

I only smiled.

An hour later there was still no sign of Peacie. My mother told me to call Mrs. Gruder, but I said I could take care of things. I could bathe my mother; I could feed her; I could dress her. When it came time to transfer her to the wheelchair, I could even do that if I had to. "Go over and see if Riley could help," my mother said. "Tell him I'll be ready to be moved in an hour."

When I knocked on Riley's door, I heard him moving about inside. Then the door opened a crack and he peered out. I held up my hand. "Hey."

"You got an emergency?" He was wearing his underwear, and his hair was sticking straight up.

"No, sir," I said. "But we were wondering if you could just help get my mother up into the wheelchair in about an hour."

"She going to the hospital again?"

"No, sir. It's just that Peacie hasn't come yet this morning, and I need a little help transferring her."

"What happened to Peacie?"

"Nothing. She just had a doctor's appointment." I wasn't sure why I was lying. But I trusted the impulse.

I went back home and got my mother and myself ready. I did a pretty good job on her makeup; she said it was as good as Peacie did, though both of us knew it wasn't. She let me wear some of her pink lipstick, and I tied one of her scarves in my hair. We looked as good as we could, but beneath this veneer, our worry was beginning to show.

When the doorbell rang, I ushered in two middle-aged men dressed in suits: Jack Peterson, the photographer, and Bill Hartman, the representative assigned to deliver to my mother a check for that astonishing amount. I could tell that they were affected by the surroundings—their soft, nervous smiles, their inability to maintain eye contact. I was always reminded of our poverty whenever someone from outside our element first came into our house, was always newly ashamed. When the men came into the dining room to meet my mother, the photographer nearly dropped his camera; it quite literally slid down in his hand. But then my mother smiled.

At three in the afternoon, Peacie finally showed up. My mother was back in bed, though awake, and I was sitting beside her, the check in my hand. "I'm sorry," Peacie began, and my mother said, "It's all right. It's fine. What happened?"

Peacie sat in the chair by my mother's bed and stared into her lap for a long while. Then she looked up and said, "LaRue in jail. He beat up pretty bad. Somebody in there with him got out, and LaRue ax him come tell me. They wouldn't let LaRue call nobody. They accuse him hiding a concealed weapon. He ain't had no weapon! They just round up the marchers they can catch and use them teach the ones get away a lesson. LaRue hurt bad in the stomach and the back, and he can't see out one eye, but he just sitting there, ain't no doctor come to see him. He ain't hardly eating. He peeing blood. I got to go there, I just hope he ain't died, time I get there. I got some things I got to say. I just want to see him." She swallowed hugely. "Now, I called my sister, she can't take care of you. I called some other folks, too. I'm sorry, Paige, I can't find nobody. But I got to go."

"Of course you do," my mother said. "But Peacie, there must be bail set. We can get him out."

"Bail set at five hundred dollars," Peacie said. "Might as well be the moon."

"What a coincidence, the moon came today," my mother said. "Moon walked right up the steps and handed me a check."

"I can't do that," Peacie said. "I can't take your prize money."

"It's not mine," my mother said. "It's ours."

I saw new clothes rising up in the sky as though they were going to heaven. I saw my beautiful canopied bed, a new washer and refrigerator, fancy shampoos, all fading away. But also I saw LaRue's warm brown eyes. I saw him sitting in jail, erect and proud, but hurting. Waiting with his hat on; I so hoped he had his hat on.

"Diana," my mother said. "I want you to go and ask Riley to come stay with me. Get me a pen and I'll sign that check. Then go to the bank with Peacie and get it cashed."

Cashed! I'd be like Scrooge McDuck; I'd need a wheelbarrow for all that money—a vault!

"Give a thousand of it to Peacie; bring me the rest."

Peacie gasped. "No, Paige! I ain't taking it!"

That's right, I thought. It was too much!

"Peacie," my mother said. "Please come here and sit by me." Peacie moved reluctantly to my mother's bedside and sat down. My mother looked over at me. "You go on now, Diana. Tell Riley I'm going to need him in a few minutes for about an hour, then take a walk around the block."

I stood still. "Go," she said. "Once around the block."

Still I did not move. *"Go!"* my mother said, and I went, letting the screen door slam behind me. On the porch I saw Peacie's small suitcase, and I kicked it over.

I went back to Riley's house and told him what my mother had said. Then I walked around our crummy neighborhood, full of crummy houses and crummy yards, crummy laundry on crummy lines, and I was angry. Why would my mother give away nearly half of what we had just gotten? Why? We needed that money! Peacie knew that! Peacie saw that it was wrong to take it! Why didn't my mother?

By the time I got back, Peacie was waiting at the door. "Let's go," she said. I looked up into her face. Nothing in her expression told me anything I needed to know. Reluctantly, I set out alongside her.

Halfway to the bank, I asked Peacie, "What's wrong with LaRue's eye?"

"I don't know."

"Will he go blind?" She didn't answer. I looked out across a field we were passing, closed one eye. "Nah," I said, answering my own question. "He isn't going to go blind. He's going to be fine."

"I just need to get there," Peacie said. "I hope that bus run on time, I got to get there."

"Peacie?"

She kept walking.

"Peacie?"

She turned to look at me, weariness in her eyes.

"I just want you to know you don't have to worry at all about my mother. I'll take care of her. I really will. I know how, and I'll get help when I need it. It won't be as good as you, but she'll be all right. You just worry about you and LaRue, and don't even think about us. We'll be fine."

Peacie smiled, a halfhearted thing, but exceptional under the circumstances. "Well, looky here. Look who done growed up overnight." I reached over to hug her, but she stepped away and looked sideways at me. "Keep those grabbers to yourself. You want me cry a river like you?"

Outside the bank, I handed Peacie ten one-hundred-dollar bills. Her bottom lip trembled as she put the money in her purse; she would not look at me. Then she walked off toward the bus stop, turning around only once to say, "Tell your mama I call her."

The rest of the money I clenched in my fist, and I stuck that fist in the waistband of my shorts as I set out toward home. Every few steps I took, I looked behind me, just in case. It wasn't a fine feeling, having so much money, after all. It made your stomach hurt. It made you worried and suspicious. It made you feel captured.

My mother asked Mrs. Gruder to change her hours so that she would be with us from nine to five. Her husband, Otto, strenuously objected to this, saying it was too many hours, so she offered us eleven to four, but just for two weeks. We took it, hoping that Peacie would be back by then. I began helping my mother both in the mornings and at night, and I began making dinner.

I knew how to make a lot of things; creating easy suppers posed no particular challenge. The challenge was, my mother felt that in Peacie's absence she needed to supervise me. She would have me unplug her and push her into the kitchen, where she watched every move I made. The way she used to do things and the way I did them were at odds, and she was constantly correcting me. My hamburger patties were too fat. I didn't let the water boil hard enough before I put the noodles in. Greens needed to be washed more thoroughly than I did it; tomatoes for salad needed to be cut into eighths, not fourths. It got so that I dreaded this time of day more than anything. "You don't cut onions that way," she said one night when I was making a meat loaf.

I continued chopping.

"Diana."

"What." I didn't look up.

"You don't chop onions that way!"

"What *difference* does it make!" I shouted. "Who cares how you do it as long as they get cut into little pieces! Why don't you just leave me alone! I know how to do this; I don't need your help!"

She gulped down some air. "I'm trying to teach you something," she said. "My way is better. And it's safer. If you keep your fingers—"

"I'm *fine*!"

"Diana, put that goddamn knife down and listen to me. You listen to me. I am your mother and you will do as I tell you. The way you are doing it is wrong!"

I flung the knife down on the counter. "You do it, then. Come and get me when dinner is ready. I'll be down the block. Just come and get me."

I fled the house, crossed the yard, and stood still on the sidewalk, trying to remember how long she had been in the kitchen, how long she had been breathing on her own. I figured she had a good half hour left.

I walked a few doors down and sat cross-legged on someone's lawn, breathed in, breathed out. A woman down the street pulled into her driveway and began unloading bags of groceries. She would carry the bags in. She would make dinner. She would probably clean up afterward, too. She would tuck her children in at night.

Up in the sky above me, a flock of ducks appeared, flying in formation. They passed directly over my head, and I could see their feet tucked up under them. They veered sharply right, then continued straight on. I watched them grow smaller, then disappear.

Peacie was gone—we hadn't heard from her in days. The ducks were gone. I wanted to be gone, too, but I sat right there, my arms wrapped tightly around myself, aware of the giant pulling force that was my mother. I hung my head, closed my eyes, and for the first time in my life wished her dead. The thought came in and out of me like a needle stick, quick but painful. It terrified me. I raced back to the house and fell to my knees beside my mother's wheelchair. I was sobbing, and I saw that she, too, had been crying. "Give me your finger," she said, her voice bitter. She bit hard, and my finger bled. I went to the bathroom and washed the wound, rinsed it with peroxide, and put a Band-Aid on it. We had only one Band-Aid left; tomorrow I would need to buy more.

I returned to the chopping block, and I cut the onions the way my mother had suggested. She was right. It was better.

We spoke little while I prepared the rest of our meal: baked potatoes, along with stewed tomatoes from the bag that someone had left on our porch. When everything was in the oven, I hooked my mother back up to her respirator. "Let me rest now," she said. "And then after we eat, I want to talk to you about something."

I went to my room while the meat loaf cooked. I didn't like turning on the oven because of how hot it made the house, but I loved the smells it created. Anyway, it was my mother's opinion that if dinner wasn't hot, it wasn't dinner.

I lay for a while on my bed, imagining how happy Suralee would be when she came over tomorrow—I'd dreamed up a whole new scene for our play: The sheriff, modeled after Sheriff Turner, trips over the dead body of Debby Black and knocks himself out.

I wondered what my mother wanted to talk to me about. Whenever she made that pronouncement—and it was rare—it was because she had something important to say. It occurred to me, suddenly, that it had to do with Dell. He'd been over a few times, and she flirted with him just as she flirted with almost any man—Brooks, various meter men, her doctors, even old Riley Coombs. But something about Dell's response made her flirting with him different. It was like he was a normal man responding to a normal woman. There was a depth to the two of them together. And there was danger. If Brooks stopped coming around, it would be one thing. A blip on the horizon. But Dell. Every time before he came, my mother would say, "How do I look?" And every time he left, my mother was silent and dreamy for a while, still with him in a way.

I understood her great attraction to Dell, of course. He was so handsome, wonderful to look at, even for Suralee and me. And he talked to her in honest ways about her condition, talked to her in ways no one else ever had. Just the other day he had been over visiting. I'd been coming up from the laundry room, and I'd heard him say, "I guess having something like this happen changes you on the inside, too."

"I don't know if *change* is really the word," my mother had said. "I've thought about it a lot, obviously. Didn't do much *but* think when I was in that lung! At night, you could feel *everyone* thinking. That's when most people cried, too. . . . Anyway, what I believe is that what happened to me, revealed me."

"You mean . . . ? I'm not sure I understand," Dell said.

"Well, it made me know how I really feel about important things. I mean, whatever the diagnosis is, isn't the issue. The issue is the way the person who has it looks at it. Understand? I know that polio made me be my best self. It's funny, it seems like people need obstacles to bring out their finest qualities."

"That might be true," Dell said. "Losing my best friend that way, in football practice? That was the worst thing that ever happened to me. But I think it made me . . . kinder."

"You are kind," my mother said. "And you're . . . Well, I like you quite a bit, Dell Hansen."

"And I like you." He laughed. "I like being around you. You're nothing like what I would expect. I mean, you know, a person hears about a woman can't move anything but her head, he's not going to think of *you.* I don't know how you do it. I don't see how you stay so . . . Well, I don't know how you do it."

"It's really true that you can get used to just about anything," my mother said. "And what helps me most is that I know I have choices. I don't focus on the fact that I can't move my body; I focus on the fact that I still have feeling in it."

"You do?" Dell asked. "You have feeling?"

"Yes."

"I thought you were paralyzed. I mean, you *are* paralyzed!"

"Right," she said. "But I can feel everything."

There was a moment, and then he said, "So . . . you can feel this?"

"Yes," she said, laughing.

"How about this?" he said, and it grew quiet.

At that point, I dropped the laundry basket and came into my mother's room. "Hey, Dell," I said.

"Hey, Diana!" He pulled back from my mother. He was blushing. They both were. It came to me that Peacie had been parent to both me and my mother, and that in her absence my mother was going wild.

I didn't blame her for wanting attention from Dell, or for taking it. But I felt, too, that it was my job to intervene, to prevent something from happening that we all would regret. For one thing, Dell had said right off the bat that he wouldn't be staying long. I hoped my mother remembered that. And here was the mean seed in my own heart that I did not understand: I hoped he remembered it, too.

After I fed my mother dinner, she asked me to get her ready for bed. When I finished, I sat on a chair beside her to hear whatever it was she wanted to talk about.

"I have good news and bad news," she said, smiling.

"Good first," I said. This was our way.

"Okay. I am going to order you a canopied bed tomorrow. Whatever one you want. You find it and I'll get it. And whatever you want on it—you're getting all new linens and a new bedspread."

"I know exactly what I want," I said excitedly. "I saw it in the catalogue. And I want the exact bedspread they show, too. It's white. *Thank* you!" I couldn't wait to lie under that canopy and look up. I wondered, as long as we were talking about spending our money, if this would be the time to lobby for a few other things. It was August; school would be starting soon. "Can I . . . What about the new clothes, too? For both of us?"

"Well," my mother said. "That's the bad news. I'm going to give most of the rest of the money to Peacie."

I sat still, a half smile on my face.

"Yesterday, when Mrs. Gruder was here, Peacie called. I didn't tell you about it until now because I wanted to think about what I wanted to do. But I've decided.

"LaRue is out of jail, but he's in the hospital. Peacie's going to need a lot more money for him to stay in there longer, and for him to get the kind of care he deserves."

"Is he blind in that eye?" I asked.

"No."

I stood up and my chair fell backward. "Then why do they need the money?!"

"Diana. The eye was the least of his problems. His kidney—"

"Why can't somebody else help? *I* won that money! Why do you get to decide to give away everything?"

"Because it's the right thing to do, Diana. And I'm not giving it all away; I'm going to keep some."

"How much?" I asked.

Quietly, she said, "Five hundred dollars."

"That's nothing!"

"Diana. If they had told us on that day that we'd won five hundred dollars, how would you have felt?"

I didn't answer.

"You'd have been so happy. Right?"

I shrugged.

"Right?" she insisted.

"I guess," I said. "But—"

"So be happy," my mother said.

I stared at the floor, listened to the rhythmic noises of my mother's respirator. Then she called my name and I looked up. "I have made a mistake," she said, and I closed my eyes, grateful. She would keep the money after all. But what she said is, "I have tried to protect you from the hardness of the world outside. I did that because I thought that with me, you have enough to bear. But you need to know something. Yesterday, those missing civil rights workers were found murdered. Those young boys."

How to respond? I felt bad, but those boys had been asking for trouble, hadn't they? Hadn't they been warned? "But . . . what does that have to do with us?" I asked.

My mother stayed silent for a long time. Then she said, "You know, it's ironic. I am in a wheelchair, paralyzed from the neck down. But I am freer than Peacie and LaRue."

"What do you mean?" But I knew the answer to my own question. Peacie's bent back before the sheriff. LaRue's order to report to the sheriff, as though he were a dog being jerked by the leash. The segregation I witnessed everywhere and that was as natural to me as the water I drank and the air I breathed. Adults I was meant to admire and emulate treated Negroes as inferiors, and I had believed it was right. But it wasn't. I'd begun learning that when LaRue talked about the Freedom Schools and I saw the brightness in his eyes, the lift.

"I can't march," my mother said. "I can't go out and help Negroes register to vote. But I can give money to LaRue, who's doing it for me."

"But LaRue isn't doing it for you," I said. "He's doing it for himself, and his people."

"He's doing it for all of us," my mother said. "I hope you'll come to see that. I hope you'll come to be proud that we helped."

"But we need help, too! We need it for a different reason, but we need it as much as they do."

"I don't think so," my mother said. "Oh, Diana. Money's just money. Once you have shelter from the elements and clothes to wear and food to eat, it's all just one-upsmanship, that's all—status and game-playing. Whose house is bigger? Whose clothes are nicer? Whose car is shiniest? What difference does it make, really?"

I said nothing. Maybe she was right. I thought about those three young men, about what had been in their wallets. I wondered if they knew they were going to die, and if, in their last moments, they stood up tall inside themselves and felt not alone. I hoped so. I hoped so. But I acknowledged, too, the drag in my heart, my utter weariness at the way we would have to continue to live. There was only so much a canopy could do.

Later I would call Suralee. She would be outraged. In trying to explain my mother's way of thinking to her, perhaps I would come to understand it better myself.

That night, rummaging around in my closet for shoes that might be good enough to start school with, I found the sheet music for a song my mother had written long ago. It was called "Sugar Bee Tree," and it had a catchy melody and good lyrics—to my mind, anyway. My mother used to sing it to me when I was little. I sat on the floor, staring at the notes my mother had so carefully penned in, thinking of all the things she might have done if she'd not been stricken with polio. She was so smart; she'd been able to sing and dance, and she'd been a really good artist, too. Even now she sometimes held a paintbrush between her teeth to do little still lifes, and once she'd painted a beribboned bouquet on a glass for me. It sat on my dresser top now, half filled with pennies.

I dusted off the sheet music and sang a line near the end of the song softly to myself. *And if you come to see, that you could be with me. . . .* It was a good song, and now it lay forgotten on the floor of a closet.

I went over to my desk and pulled out a fresh piece of paper. *Dear Elvis,* I wrote. This was his last chance.

Late one afternoon, Suralee and I were under the porch drinking Cokes into which we'd thrown handfuls of peanuts and raisins. I was going to make chili and corn bread for dinner, and Suralee was going to stay and help me cook. Dell was over visiting my mother again. She'd been outside sunbathing when he came, and he'd helped bring her in. It was so easy with him—he simply disconnected her from her vent hose and carried her, and I trundled along behind with the equipment. Times like this I wished for a full-time male caretaker, someone capable of both effortlessly lifting my mother and fixing things. Someone whose presence made for a nonspecific but very comforting sense of safety.

I made iced tea for my mother and Dell; he would help her drink it, and Suralee and I had been given an hour free.

We'd told my mother we were going to Suralee's house, but then decided it might be more interesting to eavesdrop. I'd told Suralee about times I'd listened in on Dell and my mother before, about the frankness of their talks. Now we sat quietly, heads cocked in the direction of their conversation.

It wasn't easy to hear—the sound of the fan in the open window interfered. But we did hear Dell say, "Diana and Suralee are gone, right?"

Suralee put her hand on my arm and squeezed. "What?" I whispered. "What is it?"

"Shhhhh! *Lis*ten!"

". . . over at Suralee's," my mother was saying. "You can call and tell them to come back if you need to go."

"I don't want to go," Dell said. "That's not what I was thinking. That's the last thing I was thinking. I was wondering if . . . How long are they going to be gone?"

"Long enough," my mother said. A long pause and then, "You can take me out of this. I'm okay for at least an hour." I heard the abrupt silence that always followed her respirator being turned off, the sound of Dell's steps, and then no noise at all but for the fan.

Suralee looked over at me, triumphant. I shrugged, a sudden coldness inside. "Let's go in the backyard," she whispered, and I shook my head no. "Come on!" she said, and I ignored her.

She crawled out from under the porch, and I unwillingly followed her around to the side of the house, to a spot in the bushes beneath my mother's bedroom window.

Once I'd seen a neighbor girl riding her bike down the street past my house. I waved at her and thought, *As soon as she waves back, she's going to fall down.* And she did. I started to go over and help her, but she hopped back onto her bike, embarrassed, and rode off quickly, apparently no worse for wear.

These things happened to me sometimes; I could predict random events with eerie accuracy. I believed I had a bit of my mother's psychic ability. But now I wished I didn't, for I knew what we'd see when we looked in the window. And I was right. There in my mother's bed were she and Dell, doing something like what I'd seen Peacie do with LaRue. Not quite the same scene, of course. Dell had taken my mother's shell off, and she was frog-breathing, her eyes squeezed tight with the effort. Her top was pushed up, her pants pulled down. I saw the whiteness of Dell's ass as he moved slowly in and out of her. I saw his hand over her breast, fondling it, pinching the nipple. His pants were pulled down, but his shirt was still on, his boots, too. At the side of my brain, I worried about his boots getting the sheets dirty; I'd changed them just that morning.

"Oh, my *God,*" Suralee whispered, her hand clamped over her mouth.

"Let's go," I said, and pulled on her arm. But she would not look away. Finally, I watched, too. Sick. I watched, too.

What a mix of emotions I felt! The burn of shame, of course. But then I began to feel an odd sort of pride, too. Dell and my mother. Dell and *my* mother.

When they were finished, Dell fumbled to get the shell back in place. It was all I could do not to go and help him. But he got it right, finally, and when my mother could speak again, she said, "Can you put me into my wheelchair? We'd better go back to the living room. Oh, and straighten the bedcovers!"

Suralee slid to the ground and I sat beside her. We heard the sound of Dell's and my mother's voices moving away from us, and then they were out of earshot, waiting for us to come back. Suralee would not look at me, and I could think of nothing to say. Finally I mumbled, "Sorry," and immediately regretted it.

"That's okay," Suralee said. "I'm sorry for *you.*" She shuddered.

What about her mother? I thought.

"That was so *creepy,*" Suralee said.

"What about your mother?" There. I'd said it.

Suralee laughed. "What do you mean?"

"What about *your* mother? She does it with men all the time!" *She's trashy, too,* I wanted to say, but didn't.

Suralee spoke with disdainful pity. "My mother is *normal.*"

"Go home," I said, standing up and dusting off my hands.

She stared at me.

"Go home," I said again.

"You're just embarrassed," Suralee said.

I started walking away, and she said after me, "You're just embarrassed! Don't take it out on me! Your mother's crazy, and you know it. For one thing, nobody would give away prize money like that! If she even really *won* it."

I turned around and said in a low voice not quite my own, "Shut your filthy mouth and get out of my yard. You aren't my friend anymore." I watched her walk quickly away, wishing we'd gone to her house, wishing so hard we'd not stayed here. It seemed there was a leak in my life. Everything was draining out.

I snuck around front, waited fifteen minutes, then pushed the front door open. "Hey, Diana!" Dell said.

"Hey, Dell." I waved at them, then started for the kitchen. "I'll make dinner now."

"Where's Suralee?" my mother asked, and I said she'd had to stay home.

"That's too bad," my mother said, and I said yeah, it was.

I opened the icebox and took out a package of hamburger. I could smell them, Dell and my mother. I could smell them in the air. I grabbed an onion and started chopping it exactly the way she'd taught me.

A few mornings later, I'd almost finished with my mother's bath when the doorbell rang. We looked at each other. "Cover me with the sheet, and go see who it is," she said. I could tell by her excitement that she thought it was Dell, as did I. I was sure of it. I'd heard my mother on the phone with Brenda, talking about Dell, saying, "Well, we didn't set any definite date. But I'm sure he'll be back soon." She listened, then started giggling. *"No!"* she said. "I did not! Yet." She laughed again.

But it was not Dell, it was Susan Hogart, our social worker. "Oh!" I said. "Are you . . . ?"

"I didn't call," she said. "But I need to talk to your mother, Diana." She wouldn't quite look at me.

"She's . . . I'm almost done washing her."

"May I come in?"

I stepped aside so that she could come in the door.

"Where's Peacie?" She asked the question like she already knew the answer.

"Um . . . she went to get some groceries."

"*Where* is Peacie?" Susan asked again, and again I said she'd gone out to get groceries.

"Diana," Susan began.

"I'm in *here*!" my mother called.

"You might want to take a walk," Susan told me quietly, but I stood still.

She touched my arm gently. "Come back in about half an hour. I want to talk to you then. But right now I need some privacy with your mother."

I went outside and sat on the porch steps. I wasn't going to budge. After a few minutes I saw a familiar car come down the street, then pull up in front of the house. It was LaRue and Peacie. I thought for one moment that I might die, truly, something in my chest expanded so alarmingly I thought it had burst. But then I rose and ran toward them as they climbed out of the car.

LaRue had a patch over one eye, and he moved slowly, walking with a limp. But his hat was in place, jauntily angled as ever, and his smile was glorious. He put his arms around me and held me close, and Peacie put her hands on her hips. "Subdue yourself 'fore you knock him over," she said. "He ain't no movie star." Translation? We are so glad to see you. We are here.

At some point, Suralee had told her mother about Dell and my mother, and about my doing nearly all the caretaking. And this morning Noreen had called the Department of Social Services. And Susan had been, in her words, "called on the carpet." After Peacie and LaRue arrived, Susan went into the living room with them while I silently finished bathing and dressing my mother. Now all of us were sitting in there, LaRue and I on the sofa, Peacie and Susan in the armchairs, my mother, naturally, in her wheelchair.

For a long time, I'd thought it was an advantage that she always had her chair right with her. It came to me now that I no longer thought that, and I wondered when I'd stopped. Things changed all the time without your noticing. Only the other night I'd looked at my legs in the bathtub and they were no longer the legs I knew. They were longer, and my knees had become square and horsey and without scabs. You couldn't keep up with life. It was like fabric running through a sewing machine, everything slipping through your fingers and moving away from you. It was so sad and marvelous, like the whole other galaxies my mother told me about when we looked at the stars, those places we could never know and over which we had no control. Last time we'd talked about that, I'd told her thinking of such things made me feel scared. "Why?" she'd asked, and I'd said because it was all too big and it made me feel small and worthless. "Ah," she'd said. "Well then, this is the part where we hold hands." I'd put my hand in her lap and wrapped her fingers around my own. "Better?" she'd asked, not taking her eyes from the sky. "Yes," I'd said, relieved and laughing, and she'd said quietly, "That's what people are for each other."

Here on planet Earth, though, Susan was talking in her new no-nonsense voice. "We're going to have to come up with some sort of solution. All of this deceit has to stop right now, Paige. You've got to tell me the truth about everything."

"Look," my mother said. "I'm sorry your job was put at risk, but surely you can understand that the cost of twenty-four-hour caretaking is—"

"You are given the same amount of money as others who need such services," Susan said.

"And you think they're not cheating?" my mother asked.

"They cheating!" Peacie said. "I can guarantee you that! I seen it plenty of places!"

"Where?" Susan asked, and Peacie grunted and looked away.

"Where did you see that, Peacie? I would really like to know."

Silence, and then LaRue said, "Her memory ain't all it used to be. But I know she know what she talking about."

Susan leaned back in her chair and sighed. Her hair was dirty; greasy bangs hung in her face, and her skirt was wrinkled. I supposed she'd been rushed out of her house by the news this morning. "I wonder if y'all understand that I'm on your side," she said. "Do you know that? I'm trying to help you. Now, what other people do doesn't matter for what we're talking about. What we're talking about is how we can get you covered in the way you need to be."

"If I pay more for caretaking, I won't have enough left for groceries or anything else," my mother said.

"Then may I ask why you gave away a significant sum of money?"

Peacie chewed at her lips and looked down at the floor. LaRue, holding his hat between his knees, began to turn it around and around. My mother started to speak, then fell silent. My hatred for Suralee ratcheted up a notch. So she had told her mother this, too.

Finally, LaRue spoke. "Miz Hogart? Miz Dunn just loan us that money. We gon' pay it back, too, just as soon's we can."

"The money was mine, to do with as I pleased," my mother said.

"Do you have any left?" Susan asked.

"I have some left."

"Because you're going to have to pay taxes on it, you know."

"I know that," my mother said, but I believed she'd forgotten.

"You need someone here all the time, Paige. And that someone can't be your daughter. Surely you see that it isn't fair to ask her!"

"It isn't *fair,* you say," my mother said.

"No, it isn't! She's a child! She shouldn't be put in the position of having to take care of you. It's too much!"

"I can do it," I said in a small voice. "I've been doing it for a long time."

Peacie looked quickly over at me, and I realized I'd made things even worse.

"For how long?" Susan asked, and I hesitated, then said for a couple of weeks. Then I crossed my arms and stared at my feet.

"All right," my mother said. "I would like to say something. May I say something?"

"Please," Susan said.

"Diana has been taking care of me at night since she was ten."

Susan leaned back against the sofa as though someone had just let all the air out of her. "Oh, Paige," she said. "Oh, my God." She was shaking her head slowly, like she was at the scene of a terrible accident.

"I don't mind," I said. "I—"

"Diana," my mother said. She turned to Susan. "I am well aware of the fact that I have to have someone with me all the time. Believe me. And I have thought a lot about whether or not it's right to ask my daughter to help me. I've wondered whether such a bright and beautiful girl ought to have her life circumscribed in this way."

Bright and beautiful! I felt my hands draw into fists.

"I know she suffers for what she does for me," my mother continued. "I know she suffers from the very fact of my existence." Here my mother looked over at me and I looked back at her, shook my head no. "I know you do, Diana," she said softly, and I looked away.

"But you talk about fair, Susan. Was it *fair* what happened to me? Of course not. But here I am. And let me put this the simplest way I can: If being paralyzed is my fate, helping to take care of me is my daughter's. I am deeply grateful for her help. I am deeply appreciative of it. But I don't waste my time or effort feeling guilty or thinking about how *unfair* it is. If I did that—"

"Paige," Susan said. "Nobody is suggesting that you should feel guilty about accepting care that you are absolutely entitled to. You have the need and the right to be cared for twenty-four hours a day. But not by your daughter!"

"We . . . are a family," my mother said. "She is my family."

"She is a child!" Susan said. "And I cannot allow her to function in this capacity. Even if I could accept it personally—which, by the way, I cannot—I could not allow it by law. Now, I'm going to give you a week to find someone to be here at night. Peacie, are you back now? Are you able to cover the daytime hours as usual?"

"Yes, ma'am, I sho' 'nuff am."

"And Mrs. Gruder is here in the evenings?"

A silence—nobody wanted to cooperate with the interrogation. And then my mother said, "Yes, Mrs. Gruder can be here from five until ten."

"Could you come back and spend the night, just until we find someone else?" Susan asked Peacie.

Peacie spoke quietly. "Yes, ma'am."

"I'll find my own nighttime caretaker," my mother said.

Susan stood. "You may find your own if you prefer. But believe me, I'll be checking up on you more frequently. And if I find you're using your daughter in the way you have been—or behaving in any other inappropriate ways—I'll have her removed."

"Over my dead body," my mother said, her voice low and threatening.

Susan crossed the room to let herself out. At the door she turned to say, "I have to say I just don't understand you, Paige. I don't understand your philosophy. I'm *sorry,* I know you're trapped by—"

"We're *all* trapped!" my mother said. "We're all trapped in a body with limitations, even the most able-bodied among us! And we're all guided by minds with limitations of their own. You want to know my philosophy? It's this: Our job, regardless of our bodily circumstances, is to rise above what holds us down, and to help others do the same!"

"Amen to that," LaRue said. "Amen to that!"

"I'll come by again soon," Susan said.

We all listened to the sound of her walking down the steps, to the sound of her car starting up and driving away.

Then Peacie spoke quietly. "I can't stay, Paige."

"I know that," my mother said. "I know you came to say good-bye."

I was astounded. How could this be, that Peacie was leaving? And how did my mother know that? Peacie came over to kneel beside my mother's wheelchair, then leaned over to kiss her cheek.

"You be careful, driving," my mother said.

Peacie straightened and wiped at her nose. "We will." Her voice was small and uncertain as a child's.

"Let me know how you're doing from time to time."

"We will."

LaRue got up and came to Peacie's side, took her arm. Peacie pulled away from him. "Just hold on!" she said. And then, in a more measured tone, "Hold on." She stood there, her eyebrows wrinkled. Then she said, " 'Fore I go, I'm gon' make you big batch of biscuits, put them in the freezer."

My mother smiled. "That would be nice."

Peacie took off her hat, put down her purse, and signaled for LaRue to follow her into the kitchen. "I want you sift that flour fine as silk," she told him.

"Come here, Diana," my mother said. I went to stand beside her chair. "Bend down," she said, and when I did, she pressed her forehead against mine and sighed. "I'm going to solve this problem," she said. "But if I can't do it fast enough, you may need to go and spend some time with your father."

I stepped away from her, speechless.

"I know where he is," she said.

"*What?* What do you mean?"

"I didn't tell you because he didn't . . . But he's in Jackson. He lives there with his wife and a daughter, and I might need you to go there for a little while. Just for a little while, until I figure out how—"

"No!" I said. "I'm not going there! I don't even *know* him!" *Jackson! Another wife, another daughter!* Tears started up in my eyes, and I blinked them away angrily.

"Well, I'll introduce you," my mother said. "Diana. I'm sorry. I don't mean to be flippant and I don't mean to scare you. But I can't let anyone take you from me. If you have to stay with him for just a little while, it'll be better than losing you completely. Do you understand?"

"I don't want to go anywhere!" I said. "I can enter another contest. How about if I—"

"Diana, please."

"No!"

I stared into her face, as familiar to me as my own, and then ran up to my room; it was my room, this was my room, I lived here. It was too much, everything I'd heard this morning, it was too much! How could she think of sending me to my father? Why didn't she just ask him for money? Why hadn't she done that a long time ago? Did she want to get rid of me? Was it because of Dell, who, by the way, had not even been around since that last, fateful visit? Brooks had been around—he'd stopped by to bring us some groceries, and he hadn't even been asked to. My mother had asked Brooks what Dell was up to, and Brooks said he'd been real busy. Doing what? my mother had asked, and Brooks hadn't answered.

"Oh, well," my mother said lightly, but I knew how much she hurt. I'd heard her crying at night. After all my mother had endured, it was the withdrawal of Dell's attention that pained her most.

I heard a light rapping, then Peacie saying, "Diana?"

I ran to my door, making sure it was locked. "You're a traitor," I said into the crack.

"Open that door. Let's us talk direct."

"There's nothing I want to say. And there's nothing I want to hear. Just go."

"Diana, you can be mad at me as you want. But we got to talk 'bout how to help your mother."

I walked back to my bed and sat down, looked out the window at the gray sky.

The doorknob rattled. "Diana!"

If you mix too many colors together, you get gray. My mother taught me that. Also she taught me that if a boy likes you, he calls. He doesn't avoid you.

"Diana, I'm gon' ask you one more time to open this door. And if you don't, this gon' be our good-bye."

I sat immobile.

Peacie started down the stairs, and I ran to the door to quickly unlock it. But she didn't hear me do that, and I didn't open the door. Instead, I went back to my bed and pushed my face into my pillow. Then there were footsteps up the stairs and knocking again, and LaRue's voice, and I said come in, and I let him hold me while I sobbed until my gut hurt. When I finally stopped, I leaned back against my pillow and gave out a long, shuddering sigh.

"You okay?" he asked.

"I'm fine!"

He smiled, then gave me a piece of paper on which he'd written an address and phone number. "This where we going," he said. "I ain't told your mother, I'm only telling you. It's better if she don't know. People likely come here looking for me, Diana. I jumped bail. You know what that is?"

I nodded. Knowledge from Suralee, when we'd written a play about a man falsely accused of murder and on the run.

"If I don't tell her, she can say honestly she don't know where I am."

I stared at the paper. "LaRue?"

"What, baby?"

I looked up at him. "You can write?"

In his face, it was as though the sun had come out. "That's a natural fact." He tilted his head to take me in fully with his good eye. "I done learned how. Onliest good thing 'bout jail is I had lots of time to practice! Somebody smuggled in paper and pen and give it to me, taught me how." From his pocket, he pulled out an envelope. "Now, this here? This here's for you from me and Miss Peacie, only don't succumb look at it until we long gone. That's orders from Her Highness herself. Will you promise me?"

"Yes."

He put the envelope on my dresser top and then turned to face me, his hands in his pockets. He was wearing polka-dot suspenders with his yellow shirt and red pants. With LaRue gone, there'd be nothing good left here.

"You come on down now, and say good-bye proper. Will you do that for me?"

"Okay," I said. "Just give me a minute."

"Don't worry, your face done calm down already."

"Well, I want to wash up."

"All right then." He moved slowly to the door. Something was still hurting him. After he started down the stairs, I thought about what to do. Then, although he had asked me not to, I opened the envelope. A thank-you card, signed by both Peacie and LaRue, but with an extra note from LaRue in his brand-new penmanship, in his overly large and careful letters made just like they showed you when you first learned, the little curls on the capital letters: *Thank you very much for all you and your mama always done for us both. And for everything after I got in trouble. These three little words I say next is not enough but they all I know to say and most times they do the job. We love you forever. Well it is four words I see but anyway they is every one of them true.* Next, he'd written a P.S. *This here from Peacie. She say you be good now. She say you know you in my heart forever. My eyes is also on you.*

In the end, Peacie could not leave my mother so abruptly and agreed to stay for a week. She put LaRue on a bus for Ohio and moved in with us. She was edgy and distracted, but she was there.

My mother called my father. It was a long conversation, and despite my mighty efforts, I heard very little of it and Peacie would not tell me anything. "This between you and your mother," she said. "She tell you exactly what you need to know."

What my mother told me was that my father wanted to come and meet me. She said he would be willing to take me temporarily, and I could tell from the way she said it that the "temporary" part was his idea, too. She said there was an extra bedroom in his house that I could use.

On an unseasonably cool Saturday, he came. The car

pulled up—a new Ford—and a man stepped out. From the living room window I could see his discomfort—the tightness in his shoulders, the nervous way he looked up at the house and readjusted his hat. And I could see the resemblance; I could see that some of him had come into me. It made for a reluctant rush of longing. I answered the door and he said, "Diana?"

I nodded.

"Well, you . . ." He shook his head. "Spittin' image. May I come in?"

I stepped aside and he came into the hall, then into the living room.

"Hello, Charlie," my mother said.

"Paige." He was squeezing the hat he held in his hands.

"Come in. Sit down."

It took him a moment, but then he crossed the room to kiss her cheek and sat on the sofa. I followed, with excellent posture.

"You've met Diana, of course," my mother said.

"I have!" He smiled nervously at me. I smiled back, my hands folded in my lap. He had thick hair. A mole high up on one cheek. Lips perhaps a bit too thick. Once in a great while, I'd imagined meeting my father. It was never like this. In my fantasies, he'd embraced me, laughing.

"How was your trip?" my mother asked him, and he said fine. Nothing more. He sat like a statue. From the kitchen, I could feel Peacie's eyes on us, and I wished she would come out. But my mother had asked her not to. "Just make us lunch, okay?" she'd asked, and Peacie had reluctantly agreed.

"Now, Charlie," my mother said. "I know we've already talked about—"

"Paige, I have to tell you something."

My mother looked at him, one eyebrow raised.

"My wife has asked me to . . . She's decided . . . well, both of us, really. We don't think this is a good idea. It just isn't a good idea."

"I didn't ask," I said quietly, and then, louder, "I didn't want to!"

He looked over at me and smiled, a terrible, false thing, blankness in his eyes. Then he turned back to my mother, leaning forward, his elbows on his knees, entreating her. "I came here to tell you in person, Paige. I mean, I drove all the way here. I'd like to help you, but it's just too disruptive for my family if—"

"For your *family*?" my mother asked. "Let's see. That being your wife and your *daughter*?"

My father resettled himself on the sofa. "Paige, please. Just let me . . . I can't take Diana into my house. It would just be too hard." He looked over at me. I stared coldly back. "Now, I can help you with a little cash. It isn't much, but—"

"Peacie?" my mother called, and Peacie appeared instantly, fury clouding her face. She'd heard every word. "Could you escort Mr. Dunn out?"

"I'll do it," I said.

"We do it together," Peacie said.

"If you would just hear me out," my father said, and Peacie said, "Oh, I think what we gon' do is *throw* you out."

After he drove off, my mother sat in her chair staring blankly. She looked so pretty. She'd put on makeup for him, her blue hair ribbon. "I should have known," she said. "Nothing about this surprises me."

"You had to get polio get rid of him, might have been worth it," Peacie said. A moment, and then we laughed, all of us, our family.

At the drugstore I asked Mrs. Beasley if I could tape a flyer to the window. I explained that my mother was looking for some help. "Of course you can," Mrs. Beasley said. "How is she?"

"Fine."

"Bless your heart," Mrs. Beasley said. "Now, listen. I've got some paperback books. They've got the covers torn off, but none of the story's missing. You think your mother might like to have them?"

"Yes, ma'am."

"Good. I'll just pack them up for you. You go ahead and put up your flyer." She squinted and leaned closer to see it. "Oh, you've got little tabs so people can pull the number right off. Isn't that clever. And I'll tell everyone who looks at it how dear your mother is, bless her heart."

"Yes, ma'am, thank you." I began taping the flyer to the window. Outside I saw Suralee walking toward the store. It occurred to me to hide, but then I decided she should be the one to avoid me. I finished taping the flyer up and waited for her to come in the door.

She saw me right away. She hesitated, then came over to me.

"Hi," she said.

I said nothing.

"I'm sorry," she said, and again I said nothing.

"I messed up so bad. I just want you to know I'm sorry." She looked at the flyer, then at me. "Your mom needs help?"

I shrugged.

"I'll help," she said. "If y'all will let me."

I turned to face her. "Why'd you tell, Suralee?"

She looked at me, her eyes clear. "I don't know. I hate myself. I've hated myself every day since, and my mother, too. Although I hated her anyway, as you know. I didn't know she'd call and report y'all. I swear I didn't."

I held up the other flyers in my hand. "I've got to go find somewhere to put these. Do you want to help?"

"Sure. And I was just going to get a Coke. I'll buy you one, too, do you want one?"

I said I did. We walked back toward the lunch counter and our hands brushed. She grabbed my hand and squeezed it. After a moment I squeezed back.

Mrs. Beasley came over to wait on us. "What are you girls going to have?" she asked. We told her, and after she put our Cokes before us, she asked, "When's the next play?"

"I don't know," Suralee said, but I said right on top of her, "A week from today. Seventy-five cents." I was back to raising money the hard way. I would save up to buy my own canopied bed, right after I got my mother that typewriter. I'd seen it in a magazine; it was blue, her favorite color.

"Really? In a week?" Suralee said, and I nodded, confident that we could complete a script—and sure, too, that any role I wanted was mine.

At the hardware store, I saw Dell stocking shelves. I asked Suralee to tape up the flyer, and I walked over to him. "Hey," I said.

"Diana! How you doing?" He busied himself unpacking, wouldn't look at me.

"Are you ever coming over again?" I asked.

He stood still, then turned to face me. "I don't think it would be a good idea."

I felt like the air had wrapped itself around my throat and was squeezing.

"Why not?" I tried to smile. "My mother would really like to see you." Her on the phone last night with Brenda, trying not to cry.

He pushed his hair off his face. "You know, I'm going to be leaving tomorrow."

"You are?"

"Yeah, I'm heading out."

"Oh."

He returned to unpacking.

"She probably thought you cared about her," I said.

Silence.

"On account of what you did."

His hands stilled, then resumed their work.

"Why'd you do that, Dell?"

He took awhile to look at me again, then said, "It was . . . just to be nice to her. You understand? It was an act of kindness. But it didn't mean . . . I mean, come on, you know I couldn't really . . . It was just something I did for her."

"Oh," I said. And then, "Well, bye, Dell."

"Bye, Diana. Tell your mom I said good-bye."

"Okay." I'd do no such thing.

I met up with Suralee and told her what Dell had said. She nodded slowly, then told me to come with her. I followed her to Dell's car, where she systematically let the air out of every one of his tires.

"Where'd you learn how to do that?" I asked her.

"My dad," she said.

We walked back to my house together, and when we arrived, Suralee lifted her chin and went into the living room to greet my mother. I thought she was brave to do it. And I thought my mother was noble, welcoming her the way she did. Acting like everything was fine. Offering her lunch, when it was time to cut back again.

Mary Jo Crebs sat on our sofa, chewing gum and rolling her eyes. We'd hired her, but she was negotiating for more money.

"I just don't have it," my mother said. "I'm paying you as much as I can."

"Well, I saw your picture in the paper," Mary Jo said. "You won a lot of prize money."

"That money is gone," my mother said.

Mary Jo's eyes widened. "Already? What'd y'all buy?" She looked around the room doubtfully.

"It was gambled away," my mother said. "I gave it to my boyfriend, and he gambled it all away."

Mary Jo's hand flew to her chest. "You have a boyfriend?"

"Not anymore," my mother said. "Can you blame me?"

"No, ma'am." She pooched out her lips and chewed her gum some more, played with the clasp on her tacky purse, white with gold chains, the gold chipped off here and there. She wore white nurse's shoes and a white uniform, too, the buttons gapping for its too-small size. She wasn't a nurse, but rather a nurse's aide who'd recently been fired from the hospital for "an error that was no way my fault regarding an elderly man who fell out of bed, which I wasn't even there."

Mary Jo sighed and said, "All right. I guess I can work for that if you're sure my sister has the other job."

Her sister Audrey made Mary Jo look like Florence Nightingale and Emily Post rolled into one. During the interview she'd belched loudly, then laughed behind her hands. Later my mother and I would laugh, too, but during the interview I'd felt a mounting sense of desperation. My mother was more sanguine. "You don't find many Peacies," she'd said. So we'd hired Mary Jo for morning and Audrey for nighttime duty. In the end, they were the best of the meager lot we had to choose from. Caring for my mother was a physical challenge, made worse by people's natural squeamishness about her situation: She can only move her *head*! I imagined them saying at their dinner tables. One woman had walked out before the interview even started, saying, "I'm sorry. I didn't realize . . ." Another had said, "So I'd be the only one?" The only other interviewee had a dark nervousness about her, and after she'd left, my mother said with a cool-eyed confidence, "She'd steal from us; then she'd quit." *Steal what?* I wondered but didn't ask.

Susan Hogart interviewed Audrey and Mary Jo as well, and though she expressed her approval, I could tell she felt bad. "Call me right away if you have any problems," she told me. As though there'd be something she could do to help.

My trips to the grocery store now were sorrowful things. Mostly I passed by food I wanted in favor of that which I did not. Apart from shoes, new school clothes were out of the question for the time being.

LaRue and Peacie had sent us five dollars wrapped in a letter in which they promised more money soon, but they were struggling to pay the higher rent they were now responsible for. Peacie had found a job being a caretaker for an older lady named Mrs. McGillicutty (*Every time I say her name I want to bust out laughing,* Peacie wrote), but LaRue had yet to find a job.

"Things will change," my mother told me one afternoon when I sat discouraged at her bedside. In the kitchen, Mary Jo slammed dishes around. She was clumsy and careless; already she'd broken two teacups and a plate.

"When?" I asked.

"Soon," my mother said. "I promise you."

"But how will they change?" Then relief flooded me literally from my head to my toes. "Peacie's coming back!" I said. "Right?"

My mother shook her head. "No. It's something else."

"But *what*?" There was nothing else that could happen.

"I don't know," she said. "But things are going to change soon, I can feel it. Now set me up with a book and then"—she dropped her voice to a whisper—"go and help her before she breaks every dish we've got."

I believed in my mother's ill-defined optimism. And every day I waited for the happy event that would somehow rescue us. But the days marched on and nothing changed until one night when I was awakened by my mother weakly calling, "Audrey? . . . Audrey?"

I raced downstairs and saw that my mother's vent hose had come disconnected from her shell. I reattached it, then looked about for Audrey. I found her sound asleep on the sofa. I had seen caretakers sleep before, even Peacie, and certainly I had, but it was with one ear open to hear my mother. Not so for Audrey. She was lying under a pink flowered sheet I'd never seen, her head on a pillow with a matching case. Her shoes were off. I went to stand before her and called her name. Nothing. I shook her and with some reluctance she opened her eyes. Then she bolted upright. "What's the matter?" she asked, and I was astounded at her tone. She was indignant; I had disturbed her rest.

"My mother's vent hose came off," I said.

Audrey tsked, flung the sheet off herself, and pushed her feet into her shoes. "What did she *do*?" She walked over to my mother and asked the same question.

"In case it has escaped your attention," my mother said, "I am paralyzed. I didn't do anything. You didn't attach the hose properly. Now if you will step up here and watch, my daughter will show you how to do it correctly."

"Mom, she was sleeping," I said as I demonstrated attaching the vent hose. "She was sound asleep!"

"I never was!" Audrey said. "I was resting my eyes. I can hear everything from out there."

"I had to shake you awake!" I said. "You were snoring!" This was untrue, but I felt the need to say it.

She turned away from me and busied herself straightening my mother's sheet, no longer the glaring white it was when Peacie was here, no longer wrinkle-free. "I was not sleeping."

"You're fired," I said, and she turned to me, astonished.

"Don't you talk to me that way, young lady!"

"Diana," my mother said.

"What! She brings her own pillow! She thinks this job is *sleeping*!"

"Go to bed," my mother said.

I couldn't believe it. "She's no good!" I said. "Just let me do it!"

My mother looked at me with great love and sorrow. "Go to bed," she said again, and I climbed back upstairs, where I lay crying quietly in the dark. I heard the low-voiced ministrations of Audrey. Did my mother want a drink? No? Well, then, she should just close her eyes and go to sleep like a good girl. And don't be fooling with that hose anymore. For heaven's sake, didn't she know that hose was keeping her alive?

In the morning, while Mary Jo made breakfast, I begged my mother to call Susan and have the sisters replaced. "They'll learn," my mother said. "It takes awhile to get used to the routine."

"They're awful!"

"They're all we have," she said.

Mary Jo carried in a tray with toast and cereal, juice and coffee. I rose from the bedside chair so that she could sit down. She laid a napkin across my mother's chest, then said, "Here comes the choo-choo, coming down the track!" She laughed and held up a slice of toast to my mother's mouth.

"Why don't you go and have some breakfast, too?" my mother said, and I understood that I was meant to leave the room. I did so, then heard my mother say, "Mary Jo? I am not a toddler. Please don't speak to me that way again."

"Oh, don't be such a poop," Mary Jo said. "I was just kidding. I was just trying to make it fun for you."

"It's not fun when you do that."

"Not for you," Mary Jo mumbled.

"Yes," my mother said. "That's who I was talking about. Me."

"All right, then," Mary Jo said. "We can just do this plain and boring. Now what do you want first, toast or cereal?"

"Cereal," my mother answered. And then, "A bit less on the spoon might work better."

From the kitchen, I heard Mary Jo's huge sigh.

"We'll work it out, Mary Jo," my mother said, and her voice was kind.

"Well, you're *about* the most *demanding* patient I've *ever* had," Mary Jo said. "Diana? I'm going to need you to run to the store."

As she did every day. It was so she could get rid of me. I made her nervous. It was the best part of my life, at the moment, making her nervous.

Ten days later, both sisters quit. Mary Jo announced at the end of her day that they would give a week's notice, and then they would be gone. "Why?" my mother asked. I was in my bedroom, having just returned from Suralee's. Our play, I thought, was our best yet. I came out into the hall and heard Mary Jo say, "We just feel we need to move on. We might could ask around for y'all, see who could help out."

"There is no one," my mother said. "I can tell you that right now."

"Well," Mary Jo said. "I'm sorry, but that's not my problem."

Silence, and then my mother said, "Mary Jo?"

"Yes, ma'am?"

"Get your sorry ass out of my house and don't come back. I'm reporting you and your sister for gross incompetence."

"I am not incompetent! You and your daughter are impossible! Believe me, I will be *happy* to leave."

I came downstairs to see Mary Jo walking to her car, and I went into the dining room, where my mother lay weeping in an oddly matter-of-fact way. I wiped her tears away. "Thank you," she said. "Diana, I'm sorry. We are out of options. I can't think of anything to do. I'm afraid I'm going to have to give you up. And I'll have to go to a place where I can be cared for, some sort of institution. I'm sorry."

"I'll call Susan," I said. "We'll get someone else."

My mother shook her head, then smiled. "You know what? It might be better. I think I was . . . Well, I was really stubborn about wanting to raise you myself, wanting you to be with me. But maybe it was wrong. Maybe it was never fair to you. You need—"

"I'm fine!" I said. My voice was thin and high-pitched. I was terrified.

"You need to have more freedom and . . . more fun," she said.

"I have fun!"

She smiled.

"I do! I have fun all the time!"

"And you need some nice things that I just can't give you. Everything has all of a sudden gotten so much worse. Maybe things can work out again so that we can live together. But we're going to have to talk to Susan about what to do, Diana. We can't go on like this."

I stared at her.

"Would you come here?" she asked.

I moved closer to her, and she said, "Lie down with me. Put your head just under my chin, okay?"

I did, willing myself not to cry.

"I want to tell you that I'm sorry for the times I was rough with you. I wanted to raise you right, and all I had was my voice." She laughed.

"And my teeth, right? I guess I thought I needed to make you a little afraid of me, so you'd mind. Because what could I do if you didn't listen to me?

"Peacie and I wanted you to be strong, so people wouldn't . . . We used to talk about how we'd make it so that you would always walk with your head up high. And I so much wanted you to be happy." I could hear my mother's smile in her voice, and I smiled, too. "Once, Peacie brought you to visit me when I was in the lung, you were just a few months old, and she held you up and said, 'Behold the mighty Diana!' Your hands were clasped together, your feet waving in the air, and you were smiling so hard. You liked being held like that, you laughed out loud and all the patients around you laughed, too. Peacie lowered you down to me, and I kissed the top of your head and I could smell your sweet baby smell. . . . And then I couldn't help it, I started to cry, for all I would never be able to do for you. And Peacie said, 'What you crying about?! You ain't got the sense of a barnyard chicken. *Look* at this child!' "

I knew just how Peacie would sound, saying that. I, too, had more than once been compared unfavorably with a barnyard chicken.

"Oh, you were a beautiful baby, Diana. And you were the *dryest* baby in the state—Peacie never let you stay in a wet diaper more than ten seconds, I swear! But now I wonder if maybe we were wrong, if we didn't expect too much from you. I wonder if I should have done what everyone told me to and put you in—"

"We're not going to live apart from each other," I said, raising my head to look at her.

"Well, we are. Just for now, Diana."

"I'll get a job."

"Diana, you're thirteen years old. And anyway, it's not the money. We could get by on the money we get. It's finding somebody to take care of me. And don't tell me you'll do it, you can't do it."

"We still have Mrs. Gruder!"

"She's not enough, and you know that. Now let's you and I talk about some options."

I lay back down, then said all right. But what I was thinking was, *If they separate us, she'll die.*

In the morning I got my mother ready for Susan's visit, scheduled for eleven. I worked slowly, every part of me aching. My mother would die, and I would be an unwanted orphan.

"Oh, will you stop with the long face?" my mother said. "I really believe this will be much better for both of us."

"It won't," I said.

"Of course it will! You'll live with a nice family, but you'll still be my daughter and we'll see each other all the time. The only difference will be that we'll both be better cared for!" The reason my mother had no bedsores—an extraordinary thing for someone in her condition—was because she was so expertly cared for, mostly by Peacie but also by me. No one would care for her with the vigilance we showed.

The doorbell rang, and I looked at my mother's bedside clock. "She's early," I said.

My mother nodded. "Let her in," she told me, and forced a smile.

From the window, I saw a long red car. "Wow! She got a new car," I called back to my mother and then opened the door. And saw not Susan Hogart but a strange man. "Is this the residence of Paige Dunn?" he asked.

I nodded. Now what? Were we going to be arrested?

"My name is Ed Winston," he said. "And out there in the car is Mr. Elvis Presley."

I swallowed. "What do you mean?"

"Well, I mean I got Elvis Presley out there in the car, come to see a Miss Paige Dunn. Are you her daughter?"

"Yes, sir."

"You wrote him the letter?"

"Diana?" my mother called.

"Just a minute!" I called back.

"Yes, I wrote the letter," I told the man. What was I *wearing*? I couldn't look down at myself. I couldn't look anywhere but into this man's face. He was a handsome, blue-eyed blond man, a bit overweight, fun in his eyes. "Does he . . . does Elvis remember her? Mr. Presley."

"Diana?" my mother called again.

"I'll be right there! Just hold on."

"Come here right now!" she said.

I looked at the man. "Go ahead," he said. "I'll wait right here. But hurry."

I went to my mother's bedside, where I stood wide-eyed before her. "Who's here?" she asked.

I felt for one brief moment like vomiting. Then I told her that the man on our porch said Elvis Presley was in the car outside, come to see her.

"Well, invite him in," my mother said. She was absolutely calm. I might have been saying Brooks was here.

I went back to Ed Winston and said, "I'm supposed to invite y'all in."

He nodded. "Okay, good. But I need you to do something for us, honey. Can you do something for us?"

"Yes, sir."

"I'm going to get Mr. Presley, but when he's inside, I need you to make sure nobody else comes over here. Can you do that?"

"Yes, sir. Nobody ever comes here, anyway." I remembered Susan and said quickly, "Well, our social worker is coming in about an hour."

"That's all right, we'll be gone by then. Now, I'll go and get him, and then I want you to sit on the porch and watch real good. You call me if anybody starts over here. Y'all have a back door, right?"

"Yes, sir."

"Okay." He started down the steps, and I said after him, "So he does remember her?"

The man turned around, squinting in the strong morning sunlight. "He never forgot her. She took good care of his mama."

I watched the man look carefully around at our dead-as-usual street, then open the car door, and there he was. Walking on legs just like a real man, wearing only blue jeans and a blue shirt and those sunglasses, walking up the sidewalk, up the stairs. "Hi, Diana," he said.

I looked at him. He offered his hand and I shook it. He knew my name. Inside his brain were some cells reserved for me. "Thanks for sending me the song," he said.

I nodded.

"She in there?"

At last I could speak. "Yes, sir, she's in the dining room. That's her bedroom. It's the dining room but it's her bedroom and that's where she is. Right in there."

I watched the men go into the house, closing the door behind them. But through the open window I heard Elvis say, "Paige Dunn?" and I heard my mother answer, "Yes. Hello, Elvis. Long time no see." Then I sat ramrod straight at the top of the steps, straining to hear more, watching the street carefully for the few minutes he was there. I saw old Mrs. Harper come out and pretend to shake a rug; and Riley Coombs came out on his front porch and frankly stared. Curtains parted here and there, and I lifted my chin high: *That's right.* Then, before anyone had time to manufacture an excuse to come to our house, the door opened and Elvis and Ed came out and walked quickly down the steps, got into the car, and drove off. But not before Elvis touched my shoulder and said, "Thanks, baby."

"Thanks, baby," I said back to him, like an idiot. I said it back to him! After the car disappeared around the corner, I ran back inside and flung myself across my mother.

"Oh, my God!" I said. "What'd he do? What'd he say? That was really him, right?"

"That was him," she said. "Oh, did he smell good! What did he say? Well, he said his mama never forgot me. He said he never did, either. And he said he'd gotten a letter from you." She raised her eyebrows, smiling.

"Yes!" I said. "I sent him your song!"

"Yes. And he said it was too bad what happened to me but wasn't it good I could still write songs. He said he wanted to buy 'Sugar Bee Tree' and that he'd like to offer me a contract to write more songs for him."

"You're going to work for Elvis Presley?" I asked.

She smiled. "Uh-huh."

"He's going to pay you?"

"Is he ever," she said.

Epilogue

Whenever I tell people the story of that summer, it's Elvis they almost always focus on. But one of the reasons I married my husband is that he understood it wasn't Elvis who was the extraordinary one.

My mother and I moved the very next day into an apartment complex in Memphis designed to accommodate handicapped people. Brooks drove us there, with the few things we wanted to keep loaded in the back of his truck, covered by a tarp. Suralee helped me pack, vacillating between being thrilled and weeping. I gave her the glass my mother had painted and told her, "I just know you're going to be famous. I'll see you in the movies." And indeed I did; in her late twenties, she had a bit part in an independent film that did not enjoy wide distribution, but I loved watching her in the tape she sent me. We lost touch after that, but I still think of her with great fondness.

My mother was able to hire nurses to care for her around the clock. And though I finally had that fantasy realized, though the nurses were wonderfully kind and perfectly trained, they did not come close to offering my mother what Peacie had, for all those years she was with us.

We saw Peacie and LaRue infrequently, but not for long. Peacie died from a stroke a couple of years after we moved to Memphis. Unbeknownst to us—and apparently to her—she'd suffered from high blood pressure. LaRue died shortly after that, and my mother and I both believed it was from a broken heart. I took some comfort from the fact that they got to see what happened with my mother, and a lot of comfort from the fact that they died free. After we first moved, my mother had offered Peacie and LaRue a job "supervising the nurses," but they ended up opening a grocery store, and they very much liked where they lived.

Elvis never came again, but it was because of his initial generosity that my mother finally lived as comfortable a life as she did. She tried writing a few more songs, but her heart wasn't in it, and she knew that Elvis didn't really want her music, anyway. What he'd wanted was to repay a kindness, which he did in more than full measure.

My mother went back to school, saying that she wanted to make a living for herself, earning her own money. An attendant took her to classes in a van and set her up to take notes in the classrooms—she became a whiz at writing quickly with her mouth. She was a great favorite among the other students. "I'm their pet," she told me, but it was more than that. They respected and admired her for her intelligence and appreciated her willingness to listen to their problems in the face of her own. More than once my mother's phone rang in the middle of the night with a sobbing coed on the other end of the line.

My mother graduated with honors and became a counselor for quads. She lived to practice for several years and to enjoy one of the three children I have. At forty-nine, she succumbed to a respiratory infection, as we had always feared she would. The night before she died, I sat by her hospital bed not talking much, mostly holding her hand. It was a glorious night, the stars sharply clear. She could see only a little bit of the sky from her bed, and at one point she asked me to disconnect her from the vent and take her down to the visitor's lounge, where there were big plate-glass windows. By that time, she couldn't breathe for very long without assistance, and I was afraid to disconnect her. But she gave me one of her famous looks, and I did.

When we arrived, no one else was in the room, and I shut off the lights so that she could see better. "It's everywhere," she said, and those were the last words I heard her speak.

She meant redemptive beauty, I think. Despite her many obstacles, what my mother succeeded best in doing was appreciating the many forms of beauty in life—as well as its possibilities. And she relished perhaps more than any other mother could the growth of her daughter, seeing in me a part of herself set free. I don't think it's any accident that I work for the airlines, that I am regularly lifted miles up into the sky.

After the funeral, Brenda told me my mother had always worried that the gamble she took in keeping me might have crippled me in a way different from her, but devastating nonetheless. When I heard that, I joined with so many others who wish for a chance to tell someone whom they've lost just one more thing.

I pray every night. I do it in an old-fashioned way, the way Peacie taught me, kneeling on the floor beside my bed, my hands folded beneath my chin, my eyes closed. I whisper the words aloud. At the end, I always say the same thing. I thank my mother. I tell her I'm fine. I say I'm happy. I say she was right.

About the Author

ELIZABETH BERG is the author of fourteen novels, including the *New York Times* bestsellers *The Art of Mending, Say When, True to Form, Never Change,* and *Open House,* which was an Oprah's Book Club selection in 2000. *Durable Goods* and *Joy School* were selected as ALA Best Books of the Year, and *Talk Before Sleep* was short-listed for the ABBY Award in 1996. The winner of the 1997 New England Booksellers Award for her work, she is also the author of a nonfiction work, *Escaping into the Open: The Art of Writing True.* She lives in Chicago.

About the Type

This book was set in Granjon, a modern recutting of a typeface produced under the direction of George W. Jones, who based Granjon's design upon the letterforms of Claude Garamond (1480–1561). The name was given to the typeface as a tribute to the typographic designer Robert Granjon.